WRONG!

- A themed anthology -

Presented by
Creative Writing Institute

Dedication

Welcome to WRONG!

Last year's anthology was dedicated to new writers, so it seems fitting that the 2014 dedication is to all published writers.

Congratulations for not quitting, for studying when it wasn't fun, for practicing when you wanted to quit, for taking courses when you weren't sure you needed them, for accepting criticism, growing a hard shell, reading until your eyes crossed, listening until your ears hurt, and typing until your fingers bled.

Congratulations for paying no heed to scoffers (perhaps in your own family), for plowing through discouragement, for scouring the markets until you were sick of the word *marketing*, for going to conventions and joining writing clubs, for being brave enough to proudly state, "I'm a writer," and bracing yourself for the response.

Congratulations for believing in yourself when the going got rough, for bearing pride in rejection slips, for building a platform, for investing in equipment and business cards and stationery, for building confidence and making yourself known. But far and above all of these things, congratulations for your persistence, for being dogged, for coming back and fighting your way to the top every time you wanted to quit. And lastly, congratulations for finding publication and sharing

your knowledge with wannabe writers.
Creative Writing Institute proudly salutes you!

Deborah Owen, CEO
DeborahOwen@CWINST.com
www.CreativeWritingInstitute.com

CONTENTS

Acknowledgements

This collection, compiled by Deborah Owen and Jianna Higgins, contains three short story winners, two honorable mentions, and ten finalists. There are also stories from the judges and three winners from the 2013 contest, in addition to award winning authors and other invited guests, making a total of thirty stories in various genres, but all using the same theme sentences.

This year's anthology includes a bonus Poetry Section that features three winners of the Spring Fling Poetry Contest.

Without advertising, our contests would not have been successful, and we thank Terri Cummings for devoting herself to this massive undertaking.

A huge thanks goes to our publisher, Southern Star Publishing, and to Head Editor, Jay Hirst, who donated hundreds of hours to our cause.

Thank you, Jianna Higgins, for designing the cover, editing and proofreading, and to Nicky Hirst, who kindly proofread the entire book.

CWI extends its gratitude to C. Hope Clark, who took time from her busy schedule to write the informative Foreword. Be sure to read that.

Other heroes behind the scenes are the judges who gave of themselves sacrificially. They receive no reward and no compensation other than the satisfaction of doing a good job. Let not their service be taken for granted, as there would be no contest without them! Thank you, each and every one!

Short Story Contest Judges

Key judges: Deborah Owen, Head Judge - Jianna Higgins, L. Edward Carroll, Linda Cook, and Diane Robinson, and to support judges, Lin Treadgold and Emily-Jane Hills Orford.

We would also like to thank S. Joan Popek for technical and moral support.

Spring Poetry Contest Judges

Jianna Higgins - Head Judge
S. Joan Popek
Terri Cummings
Joe Massingham

And now we present Creative Writing Institute's 2014 Anthology – **WRONG!**

Foreword

I Have a List and a Map.
What Could Possibly Go Wrong?
by Hope Clark

When we strike out on a journey, we all know that the map is important, or in this day and time, the GPS. Then there's your list of who and what you want to see along that journey. Throw a few clothes in the bag, put gas in the car or pick up your boarding pass, and you're set. These days, however, travelers panic when their GPS goes on the fritz, or God-forbid, a reservation gets screwed up. We see those folks in airports screaming at attendants, ranting from behind the steering wheel, or chewing out the poor girl behind the reservation desk. They don't realize life is not a straight line, and frankly, it's the detours that become the most fun and inspiring.

We all have our story of how our maps didn't work, and it's those stories that mold us. The go-getter who sticks to the straight-and-narrow, who keeps all his appointments, meets his deadlines and crosses the finish line is not who we want to read about. We want to know about the guy who was disoriented, lost everything, thought his life was over, then improvised and came back. Both people crossed the finished line. One just did it in a more profound way, giving us more lessons to learn.

The Plotter Versus the Pantser

As a reader or novice writer, you might not realize that two mindsets exist on how to write a first draft. The mainstream advice is to plot. Create an orderly list of who does what and when, outlining each chapter, scene, or concept to maintain order, so that you don't go off on a tangent you don't know how to return from.

The Pantser writer prefers to discover the story as he/she goes. He opens with a scene, and with each sentence, line and word, he lets creativity lead him. Like floating in a river on an inner tube with no steering controls, the Pantser knows he will reach his destination sooner or later, but uncertain of who he will meet or bump into along the way. Rapids may propel faster than he wants to go, causing a spill. Trees may block the path. Rocks may knock him senseless and leave him wondering if he'll find his way home, but in the end, he'll find a way. The Pantser likes not knowing what's coming around the bend because he enjoys the thrill of being challenged.

The Plotter spends as much time outlining his story as he does writing it. He may spend months listing each pivotal moment. At a recent conference, I listened to keynote speaker and suspense author, Lisa Gardner, elaborate about what an intense Plotter she was. Always under contract, she can't afford to write half a book and realize she made a wrong turn in Chapter Two, so she spends three months outlining, and three months writing the resulting tale. She's on deadline, so like the vacationer who has only a week off from work, she contemplates where she has to be at a given time so that she not only doesn't miss her deadline, but she incorporates all that she needs in the mission.

Just keep in mind, however, that she creates her own map. That's important.

Who Designed your Map?

The younger and more novice we are, the more we tend to rely on lists and maps created by others. That's natural. Our seniors and the experienced have covered the ground before us, and it's only smart that we learn from their mistakes and accomplishments. However, we often assume that if someone went to the trouble of making a list or drawing a map, then it's accurate. Unfortunately, there are as many wrong ones as right ones. We must not only struggle with identifying the correct advice, but also grapple with whether it fits us. All too often, people don't even wonder how a list or a map came to be. Some are even dangerous.

Because we hold an all-important list or a map doesn't mean we possess the right source of direction. The problem is that these resources abound, especially online. Everyone is full of direction, saying his or her way is the only way. When we read *The Best, The Most, The Greatest* of anything, who knows if it's true? Do we even question the merits of choice? Lists are usually based on opinion, and goodness knows we understand how many opinions are out there.

Journalists, bloggers, and freelance writers

learn early on that lists make for the best headlines.

The 100 Books That Facebook Followers Read Most

The Top 10 States to Retire In

The 10 Most Beautiful People

Or this one . . . *The 100 Best Lists of All Times* (from *The New Yorker*)

We see such lists in many places, yet they're never the same ten things. How subjective is that? Yet people run around touting how they're going through three of the ten most stressful things in life, and nobody knows who wrote the list.

I prefer to define my own stress, thank you very much.

Your Own Map

We don't want to feel we're wandering through existence with no purpose. We feel the need to account for where we've been, what we've accomplished, where we still need to go, and what we have yet to complete in order to feel fulfilled. But we don't need to be so dependent on lists and maps that we cannot change our minds or adapt when unseen forces block our way.

There's a reason a car has a reverse and a pencil has an eraser. Some people etch lists and maps in granite, as if nothing will deter the objective. Some scribble theirs in sand, willing to shift and recreate as they go, evolving from the change that crosses their path. Then there are those who define their morals and general beliefs, let the happenstance occur, and enjoy the experiences that ensue.

The most important lesson I can teach is that you control most of your destiny, and you definitely control your reaction to whatever happens to you. Today my map suits my purpose. Next week, it might need a tweak. Next month, it might mean nothing because I've learned how to cope without it, or perhaps moved on to another map that holds more substance.

We can listen to advice to make our decisions, but ultimately we opt for which items to post on our list. We not only decide which highway to take on a map, but also which map to use. We can drive or be driven. The choice is ours.

BIO: C. Hope Clark is the author of two award-winning mystery series published by Bell Bridge Books and is the editor of an award-winning website, **www.FundsforWriters.com**. She lives half the time on the banks of Lake Murray and the other half on the shore of Edisto Beach, both in her beloved state of South Carolina. Check out Hope's books and her website, at **www.chopeclark.com** and **www.fundsforwriters.com**

The Devil and Mrs. Morgan

by Marsha Porter
First Place Winner 2014 Anthology Contest

As his heavy boot flew across the room, Audrey Morgan ducked behind the dining room table. The shoe bounced off the wall behind her. She held her breath, waiting to see if her husband would continue his tirade with something else to throw or, worse, with the hand-to-hand combat he favored at her expense.

The yelling resumed. "I work hard for my money, you lazy witch! I'll get what I want when I want, so keep your mouth shut!"

Audrey wasn't saying a word but she wasn't wasting her time either. She had silently crawled under the table to the very center, figuring she may not be seen there and, if seen, she had a chance to crawl away on the opposite side when he lunged at her.

She held her breath. Minutes ticked loudly from the clock on the kitchen wall. Finally, the beer kicked in for Mel and he began sobbing. "I work so hard and nobody appreciates me…" His voice faded as he trudged up the stairs to the couple's bedroom.

Audrey remained on the cold, hard floor half expecting Mel to attack her again. The sound of his heavy body making their ancient box spring creak allowed Audrey to breathe a little easier. Minutes later his loud broken snore erupted and she started to creep out from under the table.

She froze, and her eyes widened. A pair of expensive black loafers peeked out from blue trousers, blocking her exit. She sat back on her haunches hoping she hadn't been seen.

"Come on out, sweetheart," a strangely familiar voice drawled. "I feel your pain."

"Why did you come here… how did you get in?"

"While you shuddered with fear under this here table, you sent a special delivery request and here I am to grant it."

"I didn't say anything," she said.

"It was a silent prayer that Mel would die, and those prayers are always funneled downstairs, if you know what I mean."

Completely out from under the table now, she appraised the dapper man from head to toe. "You're the devil?"

Instantly he morphed into a multicolored demon with sharp teeth and shiny horns protruding from his forehead. "I just use a gentleman's guise as my front man. It gets me in places that normally remove the welcome mat when I approach. That 'feel the pain' shtick is priceless."

Audrey showed no fear of the devil in his natural form, perhaps having seen worse from her beloved. She said nothing.

"Your understated response to me is refreshing, Audrey. May I call you Audrey?"

Her mute nod encouraged him to continue. "I feel I know you very well, and I owe that familiarity to good ol' Mel, upstairs."

"Has Mel made some kind of deal with you?" she asked.

"Every time he yelled at you for asking about the bill-paying money, every bruise he adorned you with, the time he kidnapped your dog when you finally locked him out, and so many other events, were his way of showing off his handiwork to me. Yes, Audrey, he's made a deal with me and repeatedly enjoyed himself at my expense. Heck. Ten percent of what he's done to you would guarantee his basement cubicle. Tonight, your prayer just lit a little fire under me. Mel's soul is past due and I aim to collect."

"Why are you telling me about it?" Audrey asked with a mixture of dread and a niggling of hope that Mel's daily abuse might soon be coming to an end.

"Actually, Mel has proven to be quite resistant. First I gave him high blood pressure leading directly to a stroke, but he was never struck. Then I added the high cholesterol to guarantee a heart attack, but he snores contentedly above us. Finally, I threw in diabetes to help the other two along, but nothing happened. Frankly, Audrey, I don't think anything will happen without a helpful mortal hand."

"I'm not going to kill anyone!" Audrey screeched.

"Calm down. You don't want to awaken

Prince Charming, do you? You don't need to do anything. You're going to dinner at the Coral Reef. He'll be slightly drunk, of course, when he begins to choke on his shrimp kabob. When he starts coughing, send him to the men's room. Dozens of embarrassed chokers die on the floors of restaurant bathrooms every year. Mel will just be one more. No muss, no fuss and you are finally free. How does that sound, Audrey? It's a win-win for both of us," he smiled engagingly before disappearing in a sudden smoky poof.

The next day Mel came through the door waving a white envelope. "Get your fat butt in gear, Audrey, I won us dinner in the office baseball pool."

Sitting across from Mel, whose manic return home was now dampened by three dry martinis, Audrey watched the weak flicker of the candle on their table. It appeared that the devil was wrong again, because Mel just ordered a steak instead of the deadly shrimp kabob.

"Oh, and doll," Mel shouted to the waitress as she walked away, "add an order of those shrimp on a stick things." With that, the flame in their candle inflated and Audrey felt a strange coldness in the room.

Sure enough, Mel continued drinking. When the shrimp kabobs came, Audrey tried not to watch him ingest them unchewed while he laughed about some idiot at work. Suddenly his eyes bulged and his face turned red. He tried to cough, but couldn't. Audrey felt an urge to help or call for help, but then she saw the rage building in his eyes at her inaction and decided to follow the devil's original plan.

"Go to the men's room, dear. Hurry!" she urged.

Clumsily, he bolted for the men's room. She waited. Minutes dragged by and she considered having someone check on him but was afraid, afraid he might live.

"Ma'am, I'm Paul Stevens. I'm a doctor. I was just in the men's room and saw your husband on the floor… "

"He's dead?" she asked.

"Don't worry, Ma'am. I got there in time and was able to expel the shrimp caught in his throat. He's going to be okay." His gentle hand rested on her shoulder as she began to shudder. She filled with dread wondering what Mel would do to her after this.

Mel's flirtation with death seemed to improve his disposition for a week or so. After that, he added, "Why din'cha do somethin' to help me at that restaurant? You tryin' to kill me or somethin'?" to his repertoire of verbal abuse.

So vehement were his attacks that Audrey fled out the front door and hid behind the neighbor's tall bushes the next night he came after her. When he gave up, she slumped down into a neat dirt bed wondering when it would be safe to go inside.

"We blew it!" the devil whispered just a few inches from her face. "What rotten luck… a doctor needing the head at that precise moment! Well, not to worry, Audrey, I've got a better idea!"

"He's worse than ever. I don't need any more of your help!"

"Now, Audrey, calm down. He's in there right now drinking that twelve pack and eating pork rinds. He'll sleep like a baby so you can get some rest. Tsk, tsk. Those smudges under your eyes add years to your appearance. Tomorrow, he'll be tired of all this fighting and ask what you want to do."

"He never does that."

"This time he will, and you'll ask to go to the fair. When you get there, be sure he gets fried chicken and deep-fried Oreos and Twinkies. He loves anything fried! Now he'll be pretty tired after eating all that, so you'll take him on the swan boat ride. While you're floating around, he'll have the big one… a heart attack right off the Richter scale. You just wait it out. No one will be around to interfere this time."

Audrey accepted the notes detailing her part in Mel's demise. She felt a surge of hope growing within her. *I have a list and a map. What could possibly go wrong?*

Audrey was surprised at the deep sleep she fell into and even more surprised when Mel offered to do whatever she wanted the next day. At the fair, he eagerly gulped down two deep-fried Twinkies and three deep-fried Oreos as toppers to his fried chicken. An eager fellow with a strange resemblance to the devil motioned them over to the swan boats. Mel seemed happy for the chance to just lull around in the water.

Audrey steered their boat away from the

others. This seemed a signal for Mel to raise his voice. He demanded to know where all his money always went. Audrey mildly replied, "Your booze."

It set Mel off. His verbal abuse increased and he raised his hand to slap her. She crouched to avoid the blow that never came. Instead, his palm now faced himself as he clutched his chest. He fell toward Audrey with desperate eyes pleading for her help. She merely moved over to his side, allowing him to hit his head on the plastic seat she had been sitting on.

Across from him, Audrey waited and watched. He was still for a moment, then made some gurgling sounds. He rolled over so that his head and upper torso lay on the seat and his legs hung limply to the floor. Audrey glanced nervously about and was relieved to see that they were secluded from any other boaters or fair goers.

Mel's breathing was more relaxed now and she was sure he was near death. His eyes blinked open and focused on her. "You did this! You're trying to kill me, aren't you?" he growled.

Leaning up on one elbow, he reached over, viciously grabbing Audrey's auburn hair and pulling her toward him. Even in his weakened state, she was no match for him, but she clutched his hand to stop the painful drag on her scalp. As she did, he fell off the seat and his head and chest hung precariously over the water. She shifted her weight to lean the boat in that direction and as his legs flew over his head in an amazing back flip, he mercifully released her hair. He splashed loudly before sinking into the murky water while Audrey held her breath, expecting him to resurface dramatically.

Finally, she rowed back to the starting gate. The devil gallantly took her hand and helped her onto the pier. "That was flawless, Audrey! Good job!" he congratulated her.

"Well, you said he was past due, so I guess we both got what we wanted," Audrey offered with a shaky smile.

"Actually, it was you I wanted, Audrey. I already had Mel. It was just a matter of time with him. But you, Audrey, all that self-sacrifice, forgiveness and second chances. I didn't have a chance at your soul until you made that little prayer for Mel's death. I realized then, if I didn't work quick, Mel would bite the big one and you'd be lost to me forever. Now I get you both!" he grinned with glee.

"But you set everything up! You killed him!" Audrey pleaded desperately for her soul.

"Sure, you were just going to look the other way, which might be argued as a lesser sin of omission. But then you took the bull by the horns today, Audrey. I waited with baited breath to see how you'd react to Mel's little resurrection and you made me proud! Drowning... I hadn't even thought of that!"

That said, the devil flung a friendly arm around Audrey's shoulder before his laughter erupted. So loud and strong was the sound that the earth began to shake and Audrey steeled herself for the new demon in her life.

This Woman's Right

by Brian E. Staff
Second Place Winner 2014 Anthology Contest

"I have a list and a map. What could possibly go wrong?" she says, crushing and balling up the map that I had meticulously drawn, dropping it in the waste bin as she speaks.

"I knew you would do that."

"What?" she says, looking at her empty hands. "Oh, yes, well, I don't do maps, you know that. The list is all I need."

When I give my wife directions, they are meaningless until she's converted them into her own notation. Telling her to "take the third turn on the right and go left at the fork in the road" becomes "turn this way at the fire hydrant where the shifty-looking pitbull sniffs, and that way at the obese tree with the sad leaves"—where "this" is the hand she writes with and "that" is the other one, but not always. She has tried to explain to me the conditions under which *this* and *that* reverse their meanings, but I'm still not sure whether it's due to phases of the moon, quantum physics, particle spin, or feminine logic, which, as all men know, is diametrically opposed to male logic.

Her list will be peppered with references to places where she has seen three-legged cats, vandalized mail boxes, broken swing sets, smiling seniors oscillating on antique rockers, sulky adolescents sprawled on decrepit cars, bawling infants frazzling new mothers, and indulgent grandparents smiling benignly at tantrumming toddlers. This is not social commentary; these are the landmarks by which she makes sense of her environment and manages to navigate her way around it.

Watching the face of a stranger to whom my wife is giving directions is one of the purest forms of joy in my life. As she peppers the bemused person with allusions to bizarre landmarks, her hands shoot out and back—right for a *this*, left for a *that*—in a hyperactive mime show, whilst behind her back, they see me doubled up, cackling with insane laughter.

With list in hand, she breezily sets off for the IKEA store in the neighborhood that we have only recently moved to. She loves IKEA. The IKEA catalog is her favorite reading, bar none. IKEA is another subject over which my wife and I are diametrically opposed, although I do like their meatballs, but she doesn't, which nicely preserves the asymmetry of our relationship.

"I'll make sure I'm near the phone," I tell her as she goes out the door.

"No need," she calls, and is gone, with an uncanny and totally groundless confidence that she will get to her destination unaided. I retrieve the map from the litter bin and smooth it out. She really did screw up the paper with a vengeance, and it now resembles an ancient parchment or a salt-cured pirate's treasure map, which is fitting, given her adoration of the Swedish palace of goodies for which she's headed. I give her five minutes, but it's only three before the phone rings.

"It's me," she announces, unnecessarily.

"I know. Are you lost already?"

"Of course not. But when I turned *this* way at the corner where the man mows his lawn, I came to a dead end."

"What man? What lawn? What dead end?"

"Are you going to be awkward? You know. The man who's always mowing his lawn," she says, her tone of voice implying that she's talking to a half-wit.

"Always?"

"I knew you were going to be awkward. Well, alright, not always always, but very often."

"Is it Rushwood Close you're on?"

"How on earth do I know? Oh, wait a minute, I'm reversing back to the junction. Yes, there's a sign coming up. Yes, Rushwood Close. So?"

"Isn't that some sort of clue?" I ask.

"Clue? What do you mean? Don't be obtuse."

"Closes close. They end. They are dead ends."

"Oh, that explains it."

"Thank you," I say.

"Not you. It's another man mowing his lawn. Hasn't he got anything better to do!"

"You need to take the next turn after Rushwood. It's Calypso Drive. Then you take a right on…" She's already hung up. But only for another three minutes.

"It's me."

"I know. Don't tell me, the man wasn't mowing his lawn on Calypso Drive so you didn't turn there."

"Actually, Mr. Clever Clogs, Calypso Drive doesn't exist. The next road is Walsham Avenue."

I look at the map. "When you pulled out of Rushwood, which way did you turn?"

"*That* way."

"Why?" I ask.

"Because I turned *this* way going in to Rushwood, so I turned *that* way going out to correct my error. That's why." My wife has the belief that you can correct most errors by doing the opposite of what you did to cause the error. For example, eating more makes you fat, eating less makes you thin; spending money makes you happy, saving money makes you miserable, etc.

"But now you're heading in the wrong direction. Turn around, then turn *that* way out of Walsham, then turn *this* way onto the road after Rushwood, which will be Calypso."

"It better be!" she growls and hangs up. Then follows an eerily long silence of ten minutes or so. I start to worry. A great deal of painful experience has taught me that the chances of her having an eventless ten minutes navigating new territory is slim. Has she had an accident? Been carjacked? Got caught by the police for angrily speeding the wrong way on a busy freeway, yelling curses at me and the city planners at the top of her voice? But life is full of surprises, and some of them are even pleasant, because when she calls it is to announce, "I've arrived."

But there is no triumph in her voice, so I await her next utterance with trepidation, but it doesn't come.

"And?" I say.

"Well, I'm not actually *at* IKEA."

"And?"

"I can *see* IKEA."

"And?"

"Will you stop saying 'And?' in that snotty tone of voice?"

I'm not sure that three innocent letters and a harmless question mark can be made to sound snotty, but it's not worth discussing.

"If you'd get to the point, I wouldn't need to say anything."

"Well, there's a river between me and it."

I look at the map I drew, but as comprehensive as it is, I didn't think to include a river, because there isn't one between our house and IKEA, or even near IKEA as far as I know. I tell her to hold on while I resort to Google maps, but I still don't see any river near IKEA; not even a stream.

"How big is this river?" I ask.

"Well, maybe it's not a river, maybe it's a riverette or something."

"How about a ditch?"

"Alright, it's not very big, but so what? It's impassable, unless you want me to do some sort of automotive stunt and try to fly over it."

"What street are you on?"

"I have no idea. Oh, wait a minute, there's some people over there. Oi, you!" I hear her shout. "What street is this?" I expect her to get a rude reply to match her curtly delivered question, but instead I hear her shouting "What? Sinclair? Montclair? Winklair? Thin Air?"

"Did you get that?" she asks me.

"Get what?"

"Those names. Are any of them on your wretched map?"

I don't see any of them on the Google map, or anything close, which doesn't surprise me.

"This may sound like a strange question, but where is the sun, relative to IKEA?" I ask.

"It's in the sky, relative to IKEA. Where is your brain, relative to solving this problem? Have you started drinking already?" I haven't, but I soon will.

"If you tell me where the sun is, I can work out where you are relative to IKEA; north, east, south or west, which will give me some idea where you are, which may…"

"Alright, alright, I get it. Let's see. Okay Einstein, the sun is behind me and IKEA is in front of me."

"Um, well it's around noon, so the sun is in the south, which means that IKEA is north of you, so…" I look at the map. "You can't be south of IKEA. There's an eight lane freeway on that side."

"Well I know that!" she barks, impatiently.

"Why didn't you tell me? And what are you

doing stopped on a freeway? That's dangerous."

"I'm not ON a freeway, I'm UNDER a freeway."

"Why is there a road under a freeway?" I ask, genuinely puzzled.

"If it amuses you, we could have an interesting discussion as to why they should build a road under a freeway, or a freeway over a road, but will that get me any closer to IKEA? Or should I just dump the car, wade through the stream, and hike over there?"

"Don't leave the car. It could be a dangerous area."

"I can look after myself."

"I know that. I'm worried about the car."

She replies in somewhat unladylike language.

"Look, just drive until you see a street sign, then I'll know where you are."

"Right," she says, and I hear the sound of the starter motor, which goes on, and on, and on, getting weaker and weaker and weaker. And stops.

"The car won't start," we say in unison.

"Call Triple A," I tell her. "The card is in the glove box."

"But how can I tell them where… Hello? Hello? Can you hear me? Hello?"

I hang up, put the phone ringer on mute, make myself a sandwich, open a bottle of beer, and go sit in the garden. She'll work it out. She always does, and she'll get to IKEA. The gravitational pull of the place is simply too strong to resist—and she'll buy a load of stuff we don't need and bring it home, map or no map, list or no list.

Reading the Leaves

by Gargi Mehra
Third Place Winner 2014 Anthology Contest

A beautiful summer day – Nina should've been lying on a beach in Hawaii, admiring the sun-kissed waves while Jim rubbed lotion on her thighs. But no, he had flown away on a "business trip." Had his nubile secretary tagged along? What "business" did he really need to take care of on this trip? She didn't know – she almost didn't want to know.

She settled on a long drive to re-energize herself. One foot on the accelerator, windows rolled down as the wind rushed into her hair. She cranked up the volume on her radio and sang along to the beats.

Before long, the wail of a siren rose above the voice of Beyoncé. A flash of red in her rearview mirror. She groaned. Only a long drive would clear her head. All those thoughts of Jim and his cheerful secretary left room for nothing else. It had taken so long to work up a cheerful mood, and just when she had cast off the net of melancholy and thrown a shawl of optimism around herself, the lusty alarms of a police car threw a wrench in her plans. She pulled up on the side.

A well-built cop appeared at her window. "License and registration?"

She glanced up at him through long lashes. "Was I going too fast, officer?"

"License and registration?" he repeated.

Hmph! I bet he had a fight with his wife or something. She opened the glove compartment. Something green flashed bright inside the dark interior. She flung it on the passenger seat without looking and rooted through the papers for her registration. From the sheaves of papers, several things emerged. Among them were bills, junk mail and a piece of paper that read:

Wine, fruit basket, cheese

It had been scribbled in a hurry, but the decorative swirls were familiar. Jim's letters during their courtship days offered feverish declarations of his passion in similar calligraphic handwriting. She turned it over, as if the other side would offer her a clue to its cryptic contents.

"Ma'am?"

The cop's gruff voice shook her out of the reverie.

"Sorry." She handed over the registration papers and her license. He looked at them. "I'll be back."

While she waited, she sorted through remaining papers and filed them in the glove compartment. That's when she noticed the bright green thing laying on the passenger seat. It was a leaf. She'd never seen one like it before. It shone with effervescent greenness and radiated the glow of freshly plucked spinach, like the floral equivalent of a woman with flawless radiant skin. In shape, it resembled the leaves she doodled on her notepad every day at work.

She set it back on the passenger seat. The rearview mirror showed her the cop's activities like a movie. He resembled a thicker, taller version of Jim.

A flash of red distracted her. She glanced around. It came from the leaf. The veins that snaked along it like tributaries glowed bright crimson as if pulsing with energy. She examined it from all angles. How did one handle a pulsating leaf?

The cop strode towards her. She quickly stashed it in the glove compartment. Electrified leaves would be difficult to explain.

He handed her a speeding ticket. She watched him walk back to his car and start it. When he had driven out of sight, she took the special leaf from its hiding place.

One of the veins glowed brighter. She gazed at the road beyond. The leaf clearly knew something she didn't. Maybe it would lead her to Jim. Or it might lead to happiness. The feeling came to her instinctively.

I should follow the directions on the leaf and see where it takes me. I have a list and a map. What could possibly go wrong?

She revved up the engine and drove as her leaf-map guided her. She turned right up ahead, then took a left a hundred meters after a quick glance at the leaf. Traffic lights flashed green as she approached. The beating of her heart quickened in pace. Upon arriving at a fork in the road, she turned to the leaf. Left, it indicated. On and up she drove until her heart threatened to burst through her chest. One last glance at the leaf. It pointed straight ahead.

The venation of the leaf puzzled her but she had no time to dwell on it. She found herself in a tree-lined avenue with shiny new houses on either side. As she neared a cream-colored mansion bordered by palm trees, the leaf stopped blinking and the green light held firm. Nina pulled over and stepped out of the car. The house was quite beautiful, with its sloping roof and a garden out front.

The gate was open and yielded to her gentle nudge. Her white pumps allowed her to step fleet-footed across the paved pathway to the entrance. The door loomed large in front of her. She turned the handle and it opened.

Inside, a polished marble floor gleamed as though recently waxed. The door led to a massive living room with high ceilings where a glittering chandelier hung in the center. She crossed to the other side of the room, through a sliding door, and out to a swimming pool.

She shaded her eyes with her palm. In the distance, a group of women sat around a table by the blue water.

She walked towards them. As she neared the group, their strange attires came into focus. All wore bonnets and hats that tied under their chin like Regency heroines. Nina remembered seeing similarly clothed women adorning the covers of

Jane Austen novels. She never sympathized with the insufferable girls plaguing such novels– always chasing marriage as the ultimate dream.

These ladies wore large gowns with wide skirts that scraped the floor which was, fortunately, spotless white. Anywhere else, the trains of their gowns might have turned dusty. Each held cards in her hand. A wicker basket filled with fruits held center stage. Golden goblets rested on the table, and Nina wondered what they contained. Wine?

For a moment, Nina thought the sliding door she'd walked through served as a portal to the Regency world. She had fallen into an abyss of fantasy or travelled into the past where women gathered to play bridge in the afternoons, fluttering hand-fans to stave off the heat. She felt out of place in her white pants and chiffon printed top, like a vagabond among royalty.

As she drew closer, she said, "Hi ladies!"

They turned to stare at her. Almost too late, she noticed the hooked noses, square jawlines, and whiskery stubbles. Her smile faded.

One of them said, "Nina?"

She searched for the source and found it. Laughter bubbled up in her throat. She tried to suppress it and failed as a huge guffaw escaped her lips.

"Oh, Jim, you look so pretty!"

He sprang to his feet. "This isn't what it looks like."

She strode up to him. His shocked expression amused her. His eyes shone strangely, a mixture of shame and guilt reflected in them.

She leaned in and pecked him on the cheek. "Cherry-red lipstick suits you very well." With a wave, she turned on her heel. "Bye, Jim."

She didn't stop to hear his feeble response, or the excited buzz from the others. The front door couldn't be reached fast enough now. She rushed out, past the orange vase and the low coffee tables and Grecian art.

In the confines of her car, her laughter died. Her husband deserved credit for having a different fetish. Only last week, she'd teased a friend who said her husband had a foot fetish.

A flash of green jerked her attention back to her surroundings. The leaf was glowing again this time with brand new directions, to something new, somewhere.

She'd almost forgotten about it. She picked it up and stared at it. The leaf flashed its colors mutely back at her.

"Well, it looks like you know where I need to go more than I do."

The leaf lay still on the passenger seat as she drove off into the wind, to follow her destiny.

Yogatta Be Kiddin' Me

by Susan J. Nickerson
Honorable Mention 2014 Anthology

I slide my eyes a little to the left and grab a quick peek at the doctor. Tap, tap, tap, my nervous foot keeps time with the ticking of the clock as I sit perched on the edge of the proverbial shrink couch. I reach into my handbag and fumble around for a piece of gum before I divulge my inner secret.

"I'm a sugar addict," I blurt. "I'm also neurotic and a long-time, anxiety-ridden insomniac." There. I said it. I have been exposed to my core. *Now give me a magic pill and I'll be on my way.* I wait for her response.

The good doctor takes a minute to think it through. The answer will be the same. It's always the same. Once you share that you like to write, the professionals leech on it as a cure all.

"I want you to write about it," she says. "Jot your feelings down on paper, make a list of what sugary snacks you're eating and when. Let's see if we can figure out what triggers you and makes you reach for sugar. We'll start there."

"Boring," my whiny, sugar-crashing, inner six-year-old responds. The good doctor doesn't flinch.

"We need to create a new path and retrain some of those brain cells," she explains as she reaches for a pen and paper. "These cells, these

Neurons, have been reacting and traveling the same beaten path for, what, fifty-seven years now? They are totally unaware there is another way."

She fluidly writes down a handful of psychiatric mish-mash words. Amygdala. Hippocampus. Cortex. Lines tipped with arrows that point toward sugar freedom. To my mind, the end result of her drawing is nothing more than a big squiggle. How is that supposed to lead me through the heart of Sugar Mountain?

"Boring," I repeat. "Give me an assignment. Pick a subject I can research. Something more interesting than boring Neurons and stupid *feelings*."

"Okay," she says. "Let me think. Hmm, how about …"

Oh boy! Pick the jar of jelly beans on the end table, I telepathically urge. *Or those M&M cookies in the front office! I'll write about those! Or just the M&M's if you want! Anything sugary!*

"… calming yourself with yoga," she announces. I wait for the punch line.

Instead, I hear crickets. *Really? Seriously?* My adrenaline rush fizzles. Maybe I misheard. Maybe she said yogurt. Frozen yogurt. Yes! That's it! *Calming myself with fro-yo.* I scan her face for clues. Nothing. She really meant yoga.

I repeat her chilling words slowly, as if prolonging them will make them go away. "Calming myself with yoga." Calm. Yoga. Myself. Three terrifying words that I do not understand. Three words from the planet Yogatta Be Kiddin' Me. *Yoga! Phooey! It's like all calm and yoga-ee and stuff.*

"Okay!" I fake smile. "No problem!" I try not to look alarmed. The wheels begin to turn. *Cookies and brownies and cake, oh my!* At home, I position myself in front of my computer and make sure the blank document is set-up and spaced properly. I crack my knuckles and ready myself for typing. Deep breath in. Slow breath out. I have a list and a map. What could possibly go wrong?

I type the title, <u>Calming Myself with Yoga</u>. TAP! My left foot releases a smidge of anxiety. Soon, the right foot joins in. Before I know it, they're in synch and tapping out an SOS. Tiny beads of sweat form on my brow. Just typing the letters y o g a has caused internal upset. I can hear the sugar monsters as they prepare to fight off anything that might level Sugar Mountain. The chatter is not much different than Hitchcock's birds.

It occurs to me the time has come to seek spiritual guidance. 'What is yoga?' I ask the wise deity, Google, who quickly offers the answer.

Hindu discipline, aimed at training the consciousness for a state of perfect spiritual insight and tranquility.

I feel a wave of hope! Maybe I really can find a way to calm myself! Maybe there is something to this peace and tranquility thing I've heard so much about.

"So, what do you think?" I ask the inside group of chattering, sugar hungry Neurons. "Should we give yoga a try?"

Right away my monsters -- um, Neurons -- become overly excited. I can hear them. Yackety, yack, yack. They switch gears and prepare for a fix.

"Yogurt?" The boldest one asks. "As in frozen yogurt?"

"No!" I respond. "Y - O - G - A. As in *calming* ourselves with yoga."

"Haagen Daz has excellent frozen yogart!" A new voice quivers.

Yogart? Geez Louise! They've gone and changed the spelling! These Neurons turn every word, every emotion, every burning, physical pain into an excuse to remain living on top of Sugar Mountain.

"C'mon you guys. Not all can be healed with sweets. Yoga will be very soothing and it should help us battle stress."

"That's what you tell us when we devour a pint of said delicious froyo. I would very much like some yogart now, please."

Great. They're off and running.

"We love our *Precious*!"

"We should go right now and get Ben & Jerry's!"

"We want yogart! We want yogart! We want yogart NOW!"

"Okay! Alright! Chill out, everyone!" I try to calm the monsters down but my words have no power here. The Neurons are running the asylum now and all I can do is kick back, loosen my straight jacket and hope they exhaust themselves.

The feeding frenzy passes. I look at my list. Glance at my map. I know it's up to me, *the normal one,* to take control.

"We are going to create a new way of coping," I announce. "Yoga will help us create a new path and with your help, we can create a tunnel right through the heart of Sugar Mountain. Instead of reaching for gumdrops, we shall reach for love and light."

And on that very day, at that very second, a great shadow fell upon Sugar Mountain. The Neurons fell into darkness. The once bubbly, effervescent monsters muddled about, their incessant chatter reduced to words like lettuce and water. I tried to rouse them. Tried to fake them out with saccharin and aspartame, but the monsters knew, and soon I, too, had   crossed over to the darkness.

There was no love there. No light. Just a bunch of resistant Neurons inside a weak body. Sugar Mountain was not much fun anymore and my Neurons threatened to move out. I turned to yoga and meditation to help us.

"Oh Wise and Powerful Yoga. How will we live happily ever after on Sugar Mountain when there is no sugar to be had?"

I waited for spiritual enlightenment. I looked for a sign from the universe. I was the most relaxed I had ever been. Trance like, focused. And then I heard it. A beautiful sound. It surrounded me and seemed to lift me toward the sky. The words flowed over my body and I let them enter my soul.

"Hey, hon. When you're done in there, how about we head over to The Happy Cow for some frozen yogurt?"

"We'll be there in a minute!" As I stood up, a rousing cheer went up from my Neurons. The bold one, who sounded a lot like the Cookie Monster, recited their newly established daily reflection.

> *Today we will live in the moment.*
> *Unless it is unpleasant.*
> *In which case,*
> *We shall eat gumdrops.*
> *Om, Namaste.*

Pages of You

by Tricia Seabolt
Honorable Mention 2014 Anthology

That Tuesday started out just like any other summer day. Mom dropped me off at Gram and Gramps just before seven so she could make her breakfast shift at the diner. The morning was already as steamy and sticky as hot caramel. My tee shirt was damp against my back and my hair clung to my neck and temples like moss to a tree.

For the millionth time I wished Gram and Gramps had air conditioning. "Nonsense to pay an arm and leg for something people have survived thousands of years without," Gram would say poking out her chin.

"I'm burning up," I moaned, swiping the back of my hand over my slick forehead. Gram was standing at the sink looking cool as a cucumber as she wiped down her already sparkling counter with a dishrag. Gramps sat with me at the kitchen table and stared at the Sports Section.

"You young people would have never made it an hour back in my day," Gram said with an exaggerated sigh. "Come on you two, why don't you go sit on the porch so you can catch a little breeze?"

I jumped up. I loved the old porch swing with its curly cues of peeling white paint and squished down petunia print cushion. "Come on Gramps," I urged, pulling on his hairy arm. I don't think he heard Gram.

"Hmm? What is it, muffin?" He peered at me from behind bifocals the size of windshields.

"For heaven's sake, George," Gram scooted quick as a mouse to pull her massive husband to his feet. "Are your hearing aids turned up?" She stood on her tiptoes and began digging around in Gramps' ears like she was changing a radio station.

Gramps was as big and round as a polar bear while Gram was spindly as a daddy long legs. Even though Gram liked to act like the tough one, I saw the way she looked after Gramps – like Mom looked after me. I always smiled when she re-buttoned Gramps' shirt after he had done it crooked and how she never forgot Gramps liked his toast cut in triangles and not squares.

When Gram was satisfied with her handiwork on Gramps' hearing aids, she took his hand and pulled him towards the porch. "Once I get you two settled, I'll get you both a popsicle, how's that?"

Five minutes later, Gramps and I sat next to each other clutching melting orange popsicles. I laughed as a big drop landed on Gramps' belly. He chuckled, too. "Your mother will be after me for that."

"You mean my gram," I corrected. I was used to Gramps thinking I was Mom when she was a little girl. After all, Mom said we looked like spitting images of each other when she was eleven. Plus, Mom said Gramps had something in his brain that made him forget things so he needed extra reminding. After lots and lots of re-asking mom what the name of it was, I know now. It's called Alzheimer's disease.

"Yes, I meant your Gram," Gramps said, his voice soft and far away. He used his foot to propel the swing slowly back and forth. I leaned my head on his mountain of a shoulder, feeling happy as a clam. We listened to the familiar creak-whine of the swing laced with the distant whir of a lawn mower. The smell of mint drifted warmly from behind the porch where Gram had planted it for her tea.

Gram appeared on the porch as we finished our popsicles. "We're going to take a trip into town. I need a few things from the grocery," she announced, purse in one hand and paper in the other. "Here, Melanie," she said, depositing the paper in my hand. "You're in charge of the list and telling me what I need." I knew this was her not so sneaky way of making me work on my reading.

From inside the house, the phone rang. "Be back in one minute. George, there are some wet naps in my purse. Clean yourself up," she instructed, dropping her purse on the swing next to him.

She disappeared in the house and Gramps began digging in her purse. When he extracted Gram's keys, he smiled. "What do you say you and I go to the store and surprise her?"

My heart beat a little faster. I knew Gramps wasn't supposed to drive anymore. "But you …"

"Shush now." Gramps patted my head and adjusted his bifocals. "Lord knows she does enough for me."

My mind flashed with foggy, delicious memories of Gramps driving me to get Superman ice cream or for swims at the senior center pool. I remembered giggling in my car seat as he belted out the Star Spangled Banner and passed me pieces of Trident gum that Gram insisted I was too young to have.

Any protests I had about Gramps driving disappeared behind a possibility of an adventure with my most favorite person in the world. Gramps pushed himself to his feet. "Come on, before she gets back." His voice had energy in it I hadn't heard in a long time. I skipped after Gramps as he waddled toward the Buick in the driveway, looking like he had somewhere important to go.

Before I hopped in the backseat, I glanced at the house feeling a surge of electricity shoot through me at the possibility of Gram walking out any moment. Up front, I heard Gramps fiddling with the keys. "Well, isn't that the darndest thing…" he muttered.

The car was impossibly hot and the air settled in a thick foam around my body. I could smell Gramps' Old Spice that Gram slathered on him every morning.

"Why aren't we going?" I asked nervously.

"This doggone key won't work." Gramps fumbled around some more and I unbuckled and peered around his seat.

I swallowed hard when I saw what Gramps was doing. "Gramps, that's the house key," I whispered. Maybe this wasn't such a good idea.

Gramps chuckled a little too loudly. "Of course it is, muffin, I was just seeing if you were paying attention." The engine roared to life as Gramps turned the right key in the ignition. A lump formed in my throat.

I hung over the front seat next to Gramps' ear. I could see a bristle of silver hair sprouting along his chin. "Gramps," I whispered, "I think we should wait for Gram. She'll be mad at us if we go without her."

Gramps turned and smiled a soft reassuring smile I hadn't seen since I was four and he promised to catch me when I jumped in the pool. Maybe it won't be so bad. Maybe Gram will be surprised Gramps can still drive.

Gramps snatched the list out of my hand with a determined look and patted the overhead visor where a folded map peeked out. "I have a list and a map. What could possibly go wrong?"

I let his words sink in and welcomed the cool air that streamed from the vents and tingled my overheated skin. Gramps slowly began to back the car down the driveway. Suddenly a shriek that could have been heard in China made us both jump.

I craned my neck to see Gram practically jump off the porch, her arms waving wildly. "GEORGE! NO!"

"Now why is she making such a fuss?" Gramps asked calmly, as we continued our descent down the driveway. "She knows I have to get you to school." Before I could correct him, I felt a dull thud and realized Gramps had hit the garbage can at the end of the driveway. He didn't seem to notice the half-rotted cabbage, coffee grounds and orange juice carton that spilled across the cement, let alone his wife tripping over her feet as she dashed across the lawn.

A sense of excitement prickled up my spine in anticipation of an adventure with Gramps. I did feel a little bad about Gram, but soon she'd be happy that we came back with the groceries and would see there was nothing to worry about.

When Gramps got close to the end of the street where the stop sign was, I felt the car lurch forward instead of slow down. "Gramps! You have to stop!"

He seemed not to hear me as he sped through the intersection to an angry honk of a van that narrowly missed us. "What's wrong with him?" Gramps sounded mystified and my stomach twisted into a tight knot. He looked down at his watch and the Buick swerved in a big arc into the opposite lane. I gripped the seat as my protests froze in my throat.

"I think we can still get you there before the first bell, Judy," Gramps said absently. That was Mom's name.

"Gramps, it's me, Melanie. I don't have school in the summer."

"Now, muffin, you know those excuses don't work with me. Did you study for your history test?"

Desperate times call for desperate measures. I unbuckled and climbed over the front seat as gracefully as an ostrich scaling a fence. "Gramps, I'm your granddaughter, Melanie. We're going to the store. Remember the list? I grabbed the discarded list from the dashboard and waved it like a flag, hoping to get through to him.

"Stop trying to distract me or I'll miss the school." He was looking from one side of the street to the other, worry creasing his brow. I nervously buckled my safety belt and took a deep breath.

Luckily, Gramps hadn't yet made it onto the main road and had instead driven us further into the neighborhood streets that surrounded his house. Still, the world seemed to be spinning past me as Gramps sped way too fast through the congested maze of narrow roads.

Suddenly, we were racing up behind a man on a red bicycle. My breath caught as thick as cotton in my throat as I shot a desperate glance at Gramps. He wasn't even looking where he was going. Instead, he was squinting out the driver's side window muttering, "Now, where is that school?"

"Gramps!" I shrieked, fear twisting my insides like spaghetti. "The bicycle!" By now, the man on the bicycle was so close I could see the treads on his tires.

"Whoa!" Gramps bellowed, noticing the man just in time. He turned the steering wheel in a sharp motion that sent us veering off to the other side of the street and onto the curb. I screamed at the sound of crunching metal as we sideswiped a mailbox. Luckily, Gramps and I didn't get hurt, but I knew I had to do something fast.

Tears pricked my eyes as I clung to his arm. The man who had once made me feel the safest was scaring me. What frightened me the most was not the speeding Buick, but the realization that my old Gramps was gone. This confused man who had once taken care of me now needed me to take care of him.

I took a deep breath and forced my voice to sound cheerful. "Hey Dad," I said as I swallowed. "Do you think you can pull over real quick?"

"Pull over? What on earth for? We're already running late." I could see sweat glistening on Gramps' brow, despite the steady stream of cool air from the vents.

I thought quickly. "I can't remember if I put my backpack in the trunk and my homework is in it." Gramps sighed deeply and to my relief, he stopped the car right in the middle of the street.

"Can you help me look?" I knew I had to get him out of the car.

Never one to turn down helping the ladies in his life, Gramps opened the car door and heaved himself back into the July heat.

At that moment, the scream of sirens vibrated down the close-knit street. Before I knew it, Gram and an officer were at our sides. Gram, whom I had never seen cry, was sobbing as she gathered Gramps and I in her arms. She apologized over and over for leaving her keys out.

With all the commotion, Gramps seemed to forget about taking me to school. The officer helped him into the passenger seat and me into the back. Gram sank into the driver's seat and reached over to hold Gramps' hand as she talked with the officer about the minor damage to the car.

I stared at the back of Gramps' shiny head as I contemplated what had just happened, and finally felt my heart rate slow a little. Suddenly, Gramps turned around to give me a wink. That's when I knew the old Gramps was still there. He just came out when I least expected it.

The Goddess

by Deborah Owen
CEO, Creative Writing Institute

It's too late to ask now, but I'll always wonder about the details of that torrid affair. Looking back, I guess it started in the fall of '54. Jack said she was a goddess and her parents must have thought so, too, because they named her Venus. When her name popped into the conversation, his squinty brown eyes danced mischievous circles and a lopsided smile decorated his face.

They made a striking couple – he, an obvious throwback to our Cherokee heritage, and she, lily-white, topped off with short, bleached hair and a cute button nose. Jack was a 17-year-old senior when he brought her home to meet the family. Mom said, "Uh oh. He's serious about this one."

Venus was a princess without a palace. The Barbie doll of the '50's. The perfect 10. She, and her pointy little torpedoes, f-l-o-a-t-e-d through the atmosphere without disturbing a single molecule. Her little finger cocked in elegance as she sipped tea, and the whole room erupted in music when she laughed. When Jack told me the size 4 booty-twist lived with her grandma, I knew Grandma had her hands full.

So there I stood – as far away as possible – Jack's twerpy 13-year-old sister equipped with two knotty nipples and God's promise that breasts would soon arrive. With any luck, I could double-date by age 30. I was happy for my brother, but did he have to date a 14-going-on-24-year-old Miss Universe? A few weeks down the line, Jack playfully dumped her purse upside down.

"What's this?" he said, as he picked up a letter. She reached for it but he pulled away.

"From Brian Thompson? Isn't he your ex? The Marine stationed in California?"

"We're just *frands*," she said with a heavy southern drawl.

"Well, tell your 'frand' you're going steady now."

I couldn't believe he fell for that line. Much to my surprise, Jack and Miss Universe were still an item the following Easter. Venus joined us for Easter Sunrise Services that year. I wore my new polka-dotted, taffeta dress proudly, supporting it with six starched crinolines… until Wonder Woman arrived in a pink box suit with matching clutch bag, high heels, and a queenly pillbox hat. I might as well have held her hand and called her Mommy.

Her highness stayed for lunch that day. Dad was giddy with laughter but Mom didn't seem to notice. Come to think of it, I was the only one who wasn't laughing. I wore my glares with pride until Venus passed the green beans, stared into my soul and drawled, "Ah didn't get the chayance to say how beautiful you looked this mawnin'." In spite of myself, I hoisted the white flag and joined the parade.

The following morning Jack joined me for breakfast. As I munched sugar-soaked Cheerios, he approached with the cocky smile I knew so well. He was up to something. He pulled a blue suede box out of his pocket, opened it, and I nearly choked.

"Whaddaya think of this, Sis?"

My heart ker-thumped while glittering diamonds massaged my little blue eyeballs, boogied straight to my brain, danced and sang *Diamonds are a Girl's Best Friend*.

"Oh, Jack, it's beautiful, but how do you know it's what she would choose?"

"I asked her a few weeks ago. She described it to a tee and told me all the jewelry stores she would go to. I had a list and a map. What could possibly go wrong? I'm gonna pop the question tonight. Wish me luck."

And I did.

In celebration of their engagement, Mom made a steak and mashed potato supper that night. A meal never tasted so good, until Jack ambled in looking like the ghost of Christmas past. We sat with poised forks and frozen smiles as our eyes asked one united question.

After two eternities of silence, he said in a croaky voice, "Brian's home on furlough. They eloped." Jack went to his room and I didn't see him for a week. Mom served his meals, but the tray came back untouched.

I heard him pacing the hardwood floor at night and I ached to go to him, but Mom said, "Leave him alone. Give him space." I thought he needed love more than space.

On the eighth day, I thought Montezuma's Revenge paid him a visit when he hit the bathroom on a dead run, but he emerged an hour later sparkling clean, followed by a trail of Old Spice. He stood in front of the living room mirror, pulled his shirt collar up in the back, tabs down in the front, and painted on his famous lopsided smile.

"You're a good lookin' son-of-a-gun," he said to his reflection. As he walked out the door with a spur in his step, he shouted, "Don't wait up."

The car spun gravel in the driveway, and left me and my parents wondering what had happened. If we had only known. It was the beginning of girl-chasing, with as many as three dates in a single day. Chasing girls turned to gambling. Gambling turned to drinking. Drinking to drag racing. Drag racing to brass knuckles and stiletto knife fights. He wrapped two of Dad's cars around telephone poles and lived to brag about it.

Dad roared, but Jack knew the old lion had no teeth. As Mom cried and Dad raged, I assumed the life of an orphan. The first of many crises came three months later when Mom shook me out of a sound sleep at 3 a.m.

"Wake up, honey. Daddy wants you."

"Nooo."

"Come on. Up you go."

She guided me in a stumble-dazed walk into the living room. I rubbed my eyes like a baby to avoid blazing lights until I saw Dad sitting astride an unconscious Jack. Dad's arms were as white as chalk. I remember thinking, *All the blood is in his face.*

"Come here!" he bellowed.

I backed away but Mom nudged me forward.

"Know how he got here?" His voice was deafening. "A priest found him in a ditch and brought him home. A priest, mind you! I've never been so humiliated in my life. If you *ever* come home drunk like this, I swear, I'll kill you!"

Evidently, the old lion had found a new set of dentures, ill-fitting ones. Dad pummeled Jack's face with his fists, shouting with every punch, "Wake up. Wake up!" How could he wake up when Dad kept knocking him out?

Jack's limp head flopped from side to side like a rag doll. Mom's arms held me tight as tree roots seemed to vine through the cement foundation, up around our bodies. We could neither move nor speak.

Two front teeth went sailing across the room and Dad's hand spurted blood. He cupped his other hand around the gash and rolled to the floor, crying like a baby. Mom guided my dazed body back to bed, tucked me in, and left to tend her men.

The sanctuary of my little pink room hugged me as I trembled beneath the covers and cried while Dad sobbed, cussed like a sailor, and kicked holes in the walls. By dawn, the house grew quiet and I drifted into a troubled sleep until Mom awakened me.

"Sweetheart, listen. No matter what you hear, don't come out of your room. Do you understand?"

"Okay," I mumbled as I drifted off again, but

moments later I heard Jack enter the bathroom on the opposite side of my wall. When he looked in the mirror, an ugly stranger stared back with two black eyes, swollen jaws, and a gaping hole in his face where front teeth once resided. He stuck his foot through the hamper and let out a war whoop that put the fear of God in me. I heard him storm out of the bathroom and toward the kitchen where he met Mom.

Three rooms away, I could hear them yelling. My heart did triple beats as I listened through the door. At length, he barreled out of the house and peeled out of the driveway. He left us in peace until the mysterious phone call late one evening.

Mother's voice assumed a subservient sound as she said, "Yes, I'm his mother." [Pause] "Where?" [Pause] "We'll be there in an hour."

She hung up without saying goodbye, which was a capital offense in our house, and then whispered something to Dad. Moments later, they scurried out of the house and left me home alone for the first time. The next day I learned they bailed Jack out of jail, but to this day, I don't know why he was there.

In spite of Dad's threats, Jack's drinking continued and getting girls went with it. When I say "getting" girls, I mean that quite literally. Later, he told me he had declared war on all females. Like a movie star, he turned on the charm, flirted, teased, laughed, wooed, and talked young virgins into consensual sex.

Marta was one of them. Her smiles lit up the

classroom until Jack got hold of her. She held out longer than most… three weeks. I knew when it happened because he never dated her again, and that was his pattern. Unlike other girls, Marta held her dignity without backbiting, tears, or pleading phone calls, but the fire was gone from her eyes. A couple of months later she went to "visit an aunt" for the rest of the school year. She returned the next year, but I never saw her smile again.

During those months, Jack lugged souvenirs home to decorate his wall. Rings. Bracelets. Watches. Earrings. Necklaces. Scarves. He said they were gifts, but Mom learned otherwise when late night visitors began to knock at our door. I peeked through a crack and listened.

"Are you Jack's mother?"

"Yes."

"We apologize for the intrusion, but he took our daughter's watch. He said he wanted to look at it and then jokingly refused to give it back. It was a gift from her grandmother or we wouldn't bother you."

"Can you describe it? I'll see if I can find it," Mother said.

"Yes. It's a gold Elgin with an expansion band."

Mom retrieved three that fit the description. It was the first time I ever saw the queen blush. If Jack had appeared that night, Mom would have castrated him on the spot. After I peeked through the door at a few of those late visits, reality conked me upside the head. The souvenirs were virgin trophies! The collection increased. Jack became a festering household sore that came to a head, and it burst when I was home alone.

Jack stalked in, only half-popped for a change. He stomped past me as though I were invisible and came out with Venus' 8x10 framed picture and Dad's 16-gauge shotgun.

My heart leaped into my mouth and I wondered if he'd thought of suicide. I grabbed the gun barrel, but he shook me off like a flea and marched out the front door. I ran behind and took a flying tackle at his knees. We tumbled on the ground together and wrestled for the gun. He got it first, shoved me back down, pointed a finger in my face and yelled, "Don't get up!"

From that vantage point, I watched him rest Venus' picture against Mom's favorite tree, step back, aim, and… *KABLOOEY!* The whole world filled with splintered Venus. Somewhere in the distance, a girl screamed. She sounded like me.

Jack strolled back to the house with the gun over his shoulder and I tagged along to witness the future. He reloaded, stood it in the corner of the bathroom, and yanked off his T-shirt. While I babbled something incoherent through a barrage of tears, he removed a razor blade from the bathroom medicine cabinet, gazed in the mirror, and carved four-inch letters into his chest – VMD – Venus Marietta Doles. His face twisted in a strange contortion that represented more than physical discomfort. Somehow, I knew I would experience that pain someday. Blood oozed down his belly in tiny rivulets and flowed into the sink.

I don't remember when he left. I was anchored to the spot. Catatonic, I watched his lifeblood drizzle onto the floor while more slid down the white enamel, into the drain, and disappeared into nothingness. Drip. Drip. Dark shades of scarlet ebbed and flowed in various tints. Amazing patterns shifted before my eyes. Drip. Drip. I have no idea how long I stood there.

I sensed my parents' presence before I heard them. Dad was yelling in gibberish. I couldn't answer. He shook my whole body, grabbed my face, and turned it toward him. Rapid-firing questions left his lips in English but arrived in Greek. Finally, the babble made sense.

"Do you hear me? What happened? Are you okay? Where is he? Talk to me!"

I looked at the blood dripping on the floor. Plop. Plop. Tiny puddles surrounded my feet and adorned my shoes. Was love always so painful? Was it something to be dreaded and feared? My darling brother's blood on my hands. On the floor. On my feet. Dad's booming voice. "Talk to me!"

I recounted the story through hysterical sobs and Dad flew into action.

"The shotgun's gone," he said.

Mom answered. "I'll call his friends and see what I can find out." An hour later, we had the answer. "Venus and Brian are in town," Mom said, "but no one seems to know where they are. Jack's hunting them."

"Stay by the phone. Maybe I can find 'em

first." Dad grabbed his jacket and ran out. Mom sat in the corner, a mere shell that grew older by the minute. Dark fell. No supper. No phone calls. She sent me to bed early but I heard Dad stagger in and flop on the chair.

"I can't find 'im. We wait."

I pulled the covers up to my chin and reflected on simpler days when Santa brought us red rubber band guns. We loaded six rubber bands on each and dodged in and out of doorways, laughing so hard we could barely shoot. At other times, we tossed cards into a hat, played badminton, volleyball, baseball, croquet, Sorry and Monopoly. We gorged on popcorn and Mom's homemade fudge as we watched Frankenstein on TV. I never told him how scared I was when I went to bed.

Neither Mom nor Dad had to tell me that we awaited police cars. The three of us occupied our own corner of the globe, separate, yet together. About 2 a.m., a car door slammed. I flew out of the bedroom and into Mom's arms. We waited for the knock that never came. The knob twisted with slow deliberation and our hearts stopped as Jack burst in with a purple face, a blood soaked T-shirt, and the shotgun.

Mom jumped up and planted herself in front of me. Dad pushed us behind him. There we stood, three deep, with me peeping around the column of adults, air so heavy that no one could breathe. Jack stared at us and his face screwed out of shape.

"What? You're afraid of me? You think I'd hurt *you*? My own family?"

He threw the gun down and whirled to leave. "What have you done, Jack?" Mom said.

He ignored her. Dad spun him around by the arm.

"Answer your mother. What have you done?"

Jack hauled back with a doubled up fist and Dad did the same. They stood like statues, each waiting for the other to land the first blow. At length, Jack lowered his arm and the atmosphere cleared. He paced and yelled as he spoke.

"Venus and Brian are in town and I caught up with 'em. I busted the door in, looked down the barrel at the puny little things huddled together, and I thought, *I'm the king. Me. Not him. ME!* And I told Venus, 'She who will not stand with her king is not worthy to be his queen.' I cocked the hammer, and just when I was about to blow them into eternity, I realized she wasn't worth it."

"But the blood… "

"It's my blood, Mom."

His voice cracked, and Mom attacked him with one of those bear hugs that we all had to endure.

"Thank God, you're home," she said.

"Not for long. I'm joining the Marines tomorrow."

"Oh, Jack, no. Don't you see? Everything will be alright now."

Joining the Marines turned out to be a good move. He left wild. He returned tame. He left defeated. He came home a victor with a new bride in tow. That was twenty years ago. Time flies.

He and Maggie raised four beautiful children.

The oldest, named after me, got married last year and was about to make me a great aunt when life dealt us a reeling blow. Jack had a malignant, inoperable brain tumor.

Maggie hovered over him around the clock. I sat with her on that last evening, thankful that Mom and Dad weren't there. Jack had been comatose for several days.

"Grab some coffee, Mag," I said, "I'll call if there's any change."

"Thanks, " she said. "I think I'll do that."

I heard her clattering in the kitchen as I wiped his forehead with a wet cloth. His breathing was shallow. When I kissed his hand, his eyelids fluttered.

"Maggie! He's waking up!"

His lips moved and I leaned closer to hear.

"Welcome back, stranger. Tell me again," I said.

I could hear Maggie running down the hall as his lips moved.

"One more time," I said as I put my ear to his lips.

He heaved his last breath and wheezed one word: "Venusss." Maggie rounded the corner as his head fell limp.

I sat like a stone as she rushed to his side, kissed his face, and went into hysterics. When numbness set in, she said, "Did he say anything?"

I swallowed hard and said, "Yes… he called your name."

Wrong!

by Jianna Higgins
Short Story Contest Head Judge

A vibrating cell phone dragged Amy out of the depths of sleep. She checked the lit screen through bleary eyes. A call, private number, probably the hospital. Dread seeped through her veins, and she sat up. "Hello?"

"Amy Jones? This is Dr. Summers."

Her heart hammered against her chest. *No, no, please no.* "Yes?"

"I'm sorry, but it won't be long now. If you want to be with your grandmother as she passes, you should come in the next few hours."

Amy grabbed a fistful of the sheet and clenched her fist. "Okay, thank you for letting me know." She ripped clean clothes from drawers and bounded into the shower. Tears mixed with the hot water at the thought of losing the woman who had raised her. *No, Gram*, she thought. *Don't leave me. I'm not ready.* In reality, she'd never be ready, but cancer was stealing her favorite person in the world and there was nothing she could do.

Back in her bedroom, she groaned at the snoring lump in the bed. "Jared, I have to go to the hospital. See you later." A note was not acceptable, even if he hated being awakened early.

His brown eyes flicked open. "Wrong. You

aren't going anywhere without *me*." He muttered dark words as he reached for his jeans and tee shirt on the floor. Stringy brown hair stuck out at odd angles and stale cigarette and bourbon breath wafted across the room.

As Amy zoomed toward the hospital five miles away, her stomach growled. The doctor had said Gram had a few hours. She pulled into Zambezi's drive-thru. Coffee and a donut would help the churning stomach.

"Babe, I'll have a long black. Cheers," said Jared. His body language, staring at something fascinating out the window, meant *I don't have any money* or *I don't want to pay for it.*

Amy took the risk. "Jared, when was the last time you paid for anything? It's *your* shout."

He lit a cigarette and took a long drag. "I shout at you all the time, so shut up before you make me start."

In a quieter voice, she said, "Why did you have to come with me? You don't like hospitals."

"You know you're useless without me. You'll get lost or do something dumb."

Wrong. You want to control where I go, what I do, who I see.

When the traffic light turned green, Amy pulled onto Main Street and immediately realized her mistake. A red fire engine and the flashing lights of an ambulance alerted her to the accident at the next intersection. Two cars had collided, and the front half of both vehicles had crumpled like a concertina. People in uniforms bent over still bodies on the ground.

Day or night, Main Street usually rumbled with a constant stream of people milling from place to place, cars limping from one traffic light to the next, trucks decelerating, the howl of wind blowing in off the ocean. With the window wound down, Amy noticed the stillness around her. Groups of people huddled, whispering. No vehicles moved in any direction.

To her right, Amy saw a tall, gaunt man on the footpath close to her car, and how his dead-fish eyes focused on the horror scene in front of them. Deep grooves gouged his long face and black stringy hair sat on his shoulders. *Creepy*, she thought, then decided that was unkind. When she looked back at the crash scene, she saw a paramedic pull a sheet over the face of one of the victims. She looked back toward the man in the black suit, unsure why. She glanced up and down the street, but he had vanished. Ice ran down her spine.

Jared picked at skin around his fingernails. "You won't need a funeral for the old lady."

Amy faced Jared. "What? Why?"

"There's only you and her."

Life was easier if she let him have his way, but this was going too far. "But her friends will want to come. She has money set aside. It's *her* funeral."

He slapped a hand on the console. "No. It's a waste of good money. She'll be dead so she won't know, and the money will come to us. I want to take you to Hawaii for a holiday."

Wrong. You want the money for booze and to pay

off your gambling debts.

At first, he'd treated her like the most special person on earth. The princess she'd imagined herself as a child. Then as the drinking increased, so did the beatings, the control, the threats.

Bruises could be covered by clothes. That was okay. Bruises and pain faded. It was the control he demanded that messed with her head. He had slowly restricted her friends and social outings. Her world shrank more every day. Going to work was still allowed if she came straight home. Frustration sat on her shoulders and tightened her jaw. "Why do I stay with you?"

"You know why. I'm a good looking guy. I make you look good."

"Are you saying I'm ugly?"

"Nup. You're kinda pretty, but you look way hotter beside me."

Wrong, she thought. *If I left you, you'd shoot everyone important in my life and then me*. He'd shown her the shotgun and the box of bullets with her name written on it in black marker pen.

The usual panic circled her stomach, and bile rose into her throat. She'd thought many times of how to get away from him. With Gram gone, there would be nothing to keep her here. As she watched the ambulance leave with its siren wailing and orange light flashing, she made plans and ticked them off in her head.

One… hand in her notice at work. Two… pack bags one at a time and leave them under her desk. Three… on the last day of work, get in the car and drive. Four… change her name. Five… get a whole new life. She visualized a map and saw herself heading east. His threats to harm Gram had kept her at his side, obedient, submissive. Yes, he'd load his shotgun, but he wouldn't search the whole country for her. Would he? She drew in a slow, deep breath. *I have a list and a map. What could possibly go wrong?*

And then she remembered she was about to begin life without her grandmother. The thought squeezed her lungs. She continued down Main Street and turned into the hospital parking lot.

The doctor's words echoed in Amy's mind… *if you want to be with her as she passes*. She did and she didn't. As she slammed the rusting car door, birds in the nearby tree exploded into the air. She jumped and drew in a sharp breath.

"You know I *hate* hospitals." Jared dragged his feet as he followed Amy toward the entrance doors. "Why do we have to come? She's old, so who cares? Old people die *all* the time."

She ignored him and tilted her head to allow the warm sun to caress her face. "Just breathe," she whispered to the orange orb in a perfect blue sky.

Four different odors in the hospital room assaulted her nose at once--the wax floor polish squelching under her sandals, antiseptic wafting out of the ensuite bathroom, the vase of pink roses, and something unidentified that burned her nose.

"Phew, who died in here?" Jared leaned his lanky body against the wall.

Amy chewed her thumb nail as she tiptoed to

the bed. "Hey, a little respect here. This is my grandmother."

He wrinkled his nose. "Whatever. She looks like a rotting corpse, far as I'm concerned."

Amy barely recognized the skeletal body with sunken eyes and white hair spread across the pillow. She swallowed and tapped her fingers against her thighs. Complete helplessness washed over her.

"Let's go," Jared pouted. "This stink's invading my brain cells."

"You have any left?" That was dangerous, but her love for this woman warmed her whole heart. She lifted Gram's hand. Covered in purple veins and brown liver spots, it was ice cold but soft as silk. Out the window, the blue sky had deserted, leaving a mass of broiling black clouds. They hung low, as if watching her. Amy shivered.

She ran a finger across the three diamonds on Gram's gold ring, now on her own finger. Jared had insisted she hock it at the local pawn shop, but so far she'd held out. Her grandmother's words came back to her.

"It doesn't fit me anymore, so I want you to wear it. Don't wait until I'm dead and buried. Put it on now."

Amy had replied, "Diamonds are so beautiful. I'll treasure it forever." She'd known she would inherit the ring one day, but it felt weird to have it while Gram was still alive. Or was it even more special? She didn't know. She did know that time with Gram had counted down every day.

Gram's warm eyes had caressed her. "Yes,

Amy, diamonds sparkle like *you* did before you met Jared. They're tough, hard to break. They stand for strength. Remember that."

Amy wanted to get on the bed, lay her head on Gram's shoulder and inhale her love. How long she had wanted to be an adult, and now she yearned for the safety of childhood.

"Babe, if we don't go soon, I'm gonna puke." Jared's fingers danced across his cell phone screen.

She sighed. "Take my keys and go."

"Nah. I'm starving--and broke. You have to come, too."

As Amy held the frail hand, so many memories competed - baking chocolate chip cookies, digging their toes into wet sand, running from the chasing waves, craft projects on the dining table. Tears spilled down her cheeks.

One rose petal dropped onto the bedside table. The edges instantly turned up. It seemed appropriate. "Gram, can you hear me? Please open your eyes. Don't leave me. I love you so much, and I don't have anyone else." She realized how selfish that sounded.

Jared snorted. "Babe, you've got *me*. I'm all you need."

She laid her head on the stiff white sheets. "It's only two weeks till my 21st, Gram. Please get better. I can't celebrate without you."

A nurse pushed through the door. Her old fashioned, white uniform crackled as she moved. "Shouldn't be long now." She stared unblinking at the old woman.

The odor intensified and wafted through the room. Amy sat up and gripped the green blanket. "Phew. What *is* that?"

Jared batted the air. "Oh gross, lady. We could smell you coming."

The nurse nodded. "Ah yes. Not everyone is sensitive to my… aroma."

A low fog swirled around Amy's sandals, and she kicked at it. Her toes curled as the cold settled against her skin. Right then she recognized the fourth smell--rotting silage. Her breath caught in her throat when the nurse shimmered like a hologram. "Whoa, who *are* you? You're not a real nurse." Her chair fell backward as she stood and backed up against the wall.

Blood red lips curled in a smile. "I'm Death. I'm waiting. That's what I do. One minute 'til flatline."

Amy's hands clenched, and fear snaked down her spine. "You're a reaper? Waiting for *her*? But why *her*?" The image of the man in black at the accident came to mind. He looked like someone who would wait for souls. Not this overweight, pasty woman in a uniform.

"She's on my list."

Amy swallowed a sob. How could she be having this conversation? Everything was out of control. "What list? Show me."

Death reached into her pockets, but her hands came up empty. Her eyes widened. "I've misplaced it, but I can't go back without her."

Panic washed over Amy like a tidal wave. And

then she pushed it aside. "Without *her,* or without *someone*?" She was breathing too fast, and black dots danced in front of her eyes.

"If I return without a body, my butt will be kicked to Purgatory. I've heard stories, and no way I wanna go there."

"She's a good person. You *can't* take her." Amy took a deep breath, unclenched her fists and pointed at Jared. "Take *him*."

Death frowned. Without moving her head, she swiveled her eyes to Jared and back to Amy. "You sure?"

Amy held her grandmother's hand tighter and nodded.

The reaper folded her arms. "Well, he's much younger, so I'll get extra points."

Amy felt hope return and her heart beat faster. Could she bargain for a better deal? "She must be in perfect health. How long?"

The reaper pursed her lips. "She's old. Another three years."

Amy shook her head. "He's young. Big points, remember? Make it ten, or no deal."

Death shrugged as if the decision was insignificant. "Okay, done." She snapped her fingers.

Jared cried out like a screech owl, clutched his head and thudded onto the floor. A final breath released.

With little emotion, Amy pressed the red *alert* buzzer and heard rubber-soled shoes running toward the room. Too late.

Amy faced him for the last time. "Well, Jared. You were wrong. She's old, but *idiots* die *all* the time."

Gram drew in a slow, shuddering breath and a healthy pink flooded her cheeks. She opened her eyes and blinked several times until she located her granddaughter. "Amy, I'm sorry, honey, did I nod off? I feel so much better." A smile lit her weathered face.

Amy linked her fingers with the old woman's and noted their warmth. In her mind she tore up the list and map. *Not needed.* "Yes you did, Gram. You're well now, and I'm taking you home."

BIO: Jianna is the author of the *Just So* series, the *Destiny* series and the *Athanasia* series. Her books have won an honorable mention medal in the Global Ebook awards and have been finalists in several novel contests, including Readers' Favorite, the Kindle Best Indie Book Awards, and the Writers' Village International Novel Contest. **http://www.jiannahiggins.wix.com/books**

Ice Mountain

by S. Joan Popek
CWI Staff and Award Winning Author

Grandfather stared into the black night through the tiny, kitchen window. He shivered. "This cold creeps into your bones and lodges itself deep into your marrow with aching brittleness. One touch, one wrong move and you're sure that your skeleton will shatter like an icicle thrown against a brick wall." He turned. His dark eyes examined Joey from within a pale, wind-weathered face.

Joey pretended to listen, but he shifted back and forth on his chair as if his legs were coiled springs drawn taut and ready to leap into action. His feet jiggled against the floor. His excitement was a land mine ready to explode. He would be twelve years old tomorrow and on that day, his whole life would change.

Grandfather's eyes narrowed. He stopped talking, and his gaze held Joey's eyes. The boy squirmed on his high-backed wooden chair and looked down at his boots. The thin soles etched a dark brown outline against the yellowed tile of the floor. He always hated it when Grandfather looked at him like that. Those eyes made him think of two fishing holes carved into thick, lake ice. The dusky water in the holes swirled and foamed as if gathering speed to suddenly lurch out of the frozen dark and jerk warm-blooded creatures down to the depths. Right now, Grandpa's eyes threatened to jerk all of Joey's secrets right out of him.

That afternoon, he had snuck down to Old Town, a spot forbidden to all of the forty-three children in New Town. His twelve year-old spirit wouldn't let him rest until he went one last time. He had found a tarnished, gold watch buried beneath a pile of twisted, steel girders and broken bricks. Hidden deep in his pocket, it seemed to burn through his pants into his skin now that Grandfather knew he had disobeyed.

Grandpa stared at him a moment and sighed. "Son, have you been to Old Town?"

Joey looked up at his grandfather, and fought the tears that burned at the edges of his eyes. "Grandpa, I..."

"Son, it's dangerous to go there. You know that. Those old buildings can come down without warning and bury you alive. We'd never find you in all that mess. Nothing down there is worth your life. You hear? Especially now."

"Yes, sir." Joey nibbled at his lower lip. A visceral quivering in his belly reminded him of how much he hated disappointing his grandfather.

Grandpa lowered himself to his knees, his eyes level with Joey's. Suddenly, he pulled Joey to him in a tight hug. When he released him, Joey noticed that his eyes were damp, then Grandpa stood up abruptly and said, "Wish we could go fishin'."

They both knew the chances of catching anything alive were slim, but occasionally they were rewarded with a hardy fish that Joey's mom would cook into a delicious stew. The stew was usually more water than fish, but sometimes a traveler would trade a slice of bear meat or even a highly valued potato or onion from one of the few places where the soil hadn't turned to stone-hard ice.

Joey smiled. "Yep, me too."

Grandpa sat down in the wooden chair on the other side of the large metal shipping carton that served as the family's table. He laced his hands behind his neck and leaned back. The two front legs of the chair raised a bit and hovered there as if defying gravity, then gently lowered back down to rest on the patched linoleum. He smiled. "Yep. I remember when I was a kid, a lot younger than you. The mountain was a lot further away then, you know."

Joey relaxed, laced his hands behind his neck and leaned back in his chair, imitating his grandfather. Of course he knew. He tried to relax, but tonight it was hard to concentrate. His mind kept racing to tomorrow, to the adventure that awaited them.

He forced his attention back to his grandfather, leaned forward and asked, "Grandpa? Did this land really used to be a desert?" He pointed to an old, yellowed picture over the pot-bellied stove in the kitchen. The orange setting sun perched behind a rolling landscape dotted with tall, green plants that cast spiked shadows across reddish brown sand. Grandpa said the plants were called cactus. "Those cactus look like people with their arms raised," Joey said as he studied the picture.

Grandfather glanced at the picture and nodded. "Yep, they do, don't they? Course, I was just a boy, but I remember. Wasn't no water for miles except for a few narrow rivers and a lake or two. Sure wasn't no ocean. That was a thousand miles away. And no ice mountain either. Then the earthquakes started, and the tornados and hurricanes..." His voice broke and he fell suddenly silent.

Joey looked at his serious face, and a sad, inner warmth crept into him, pushing some of the chill of the room away. He tried to shove tomorrow's excitement out of his mind and gazed at the small flames and red embers in the pot-bellied stove. They were down to the last of the fuel. Mama's two beloved wooden chairs would be the last to go. He ran his fingers across the smooth edge of the wooden seat he sat in. Everything that would burn had been burned. That was what tomorrow was all about. Joey stared, hypnotized, into the fire and whispered, "Was it really warm all the time, Grandpa?"

"Well, not all the time. We had a few cold spells when the rains came, and even a little snow once in a while. Course, while I was growing up, my Pa, your great grandpa, used to tell me about really cold winters in the mountains."

"But, Grandpa, you said there wasn't any mountains when you was a kid."

"Oh, not ice mountains like those glaciers in the bay. I mean real mountains, with dirt and rocks and trees growin' all over 'em." He leaned back in his chair and gazed at the ceiling.

Neither of them spoke for a few minutes. Both dreaming their own dreams.

Joey finally broke the silence. "Must'a been something to see."

"Yeah, it was. That water came boilin' down the valley like it wasn't gonna stop. Waves hit those mountains over there and climbed right up their sides like they was just little bumps in a road. Pa said later, if them mountains hadn't been there to stop it, the coastline might'a made it all the way to Texas. He said we were lucky to be alive, even if the edges of the flood did wash out most of the town."

"That's when the first ice mountain came?"

"No. That wasn't 'til later. First, the snow and ice storms. We were still tryin' to clean up what was left of the town. It was slow goin' in the cold, but we kept diggin' through the rubble of all those collapsed buildings, buryin' the dead and findin' what food we could when the first mountain floated in." The old man leaned forward and ran strong, work-worn fingers through thinning, grey hair. He grinned. "I was one of the first ones to spot it, you know."

Joey nodded. "Yeah, Grandpa, I know." He tried to imagine what a world without constant cold, ice and snow would be like. Sometimes, when the clouds lifted a little, he would watch the hazy sun in the sky and feel a little warmer by just looking at it. One of his mother's prized books said that the sun was a giant ball of fire. He tried to imagine a fire hot enough to warm up a whole world. He couldn't, but grandfather swore it was true, so it probably was. He thought about yesterday when they had finally burned Mother's precious books. Next would be the chairs.

Mother told them they might as well have something to sit on for a few days longer, and it was only practical to save the chairs until last. She had insisted on putting the books into the old stove herself. She cried softly as she slowly tore each page out one by one and wadded them into tight, little balls so they would burn longer, then dropped them into the small blaze.

Watching her, Grandpa's eyes had glistened with tears. The books and the chairs had belonged to his mother, then to Grandma until she died.

Joey shivered at the memory and asked, "Grandpa?"

"Yeah?"

"What's a greenhouse?"

"Well, I'm not real sure. Never really seen one, but my Pa used to say they were big ol' houses made out of glass, and all kinds of plants grew in there. It was supposed to be real warm inside." He looked at Joey and smiled. "You're wonderin' about why everyone says the ice is caused by what they call the greenhouse effect, aren't you?"

"Yeah. If a greenhouse is all warm, how can that have anything to do with ice mountains?"

Grandpa chuckled. "Darned if I know, boy. I never figured that out either." His soft chuckle became a hearty, contagious laugh that Joey couldn't help picking up. They both giggled at each other like two kids with a secret.

Suddenly, Grandpa slapped his knee and sobered. He stood up, took a step toward the stove, then stopped as if he forgot what he was doing. He turned around, sat back down in his chair and continued as if there had been no break in the conversation. "My Pa knew though. He used to talk about it a lot with the other people who survived. One of 'em was a scientist or somethin'. He was on his way to California and stopped in town to spend the night. He said he was goin' to some big earthquake center there. The next morning, there wasn't no California no more, so he stuck around to help. He tried to explain it to us. All about the earthquakes shiftin' the world around, then the polar ice caps meltin' and stuff like that. He was real smart. Hooked up an old car battery to a couple of radios and tried to call for help. Nobody ever came though." Grandpa grew silent again and stared at the table as if trying to decipher an invisible code in the scratches on its surface.

Joey reached over and touched his hand. "Did you talk to other people in other places on them radios?"

Grandpa shook his head and looked up. "Huh? Oh, where was I? Oh, yeah. Well, anyway, while the radios were still workin', we got news from other parts of the world. Seemed that things were a lot worse in other places, so Pa decided to stay here, but most of the other families left town after the first glacier showed up. That scientist fellow went with 'em. Said he'd send the National Guard back."

"What's the National Guard?"

"I'm not sure. Some kind of emergency force, my pa said. Anyway, they never showed up."

"What happened to the others? The ones that left."

"Don't know, son. We never heard from any of 'em again."

They both stared at the fire awhile, listening to Mama sing to Joey's three year-old baby sister in the other room. The toddler whimpered softly in her sleep.

Finally, Joey asked quietly, "Why did Daddy go on the ice?"

"Cause it was there, I guess. When the second one floated in, he said he had to go. Maybe he was hoping to find a bear or somethin' he could bring back for food." He sighed. "He wasn't the first, you know. And I doubt he'll be the last."

"Do you think a bear got him?"

"Don't know, son. Maybe. Maybe he fell into one of them crevices. Maybe into the ocean. Glaciers are dangerous things. Almost alive. They move and groan and grow. Yep. Almost alive."

As if in agreement with Grandpa, a long, creaking moan echoed through the night as the two mountains in the bay shifted minutely and scraped against each other. Their wailing screeches sent chills racing through Joey's stomach.

"They're marching again," he whispered.
"Yep."

Joey's thoughts turned to tomorrow. "Do you think we'll find it, Grandpa?"

"Find what, son?"

"Warmth."

"I sure hope so. Last we heard, the earthquakes raised a big ol' land mass between the East Coast of America and Spain. If we go north a ways, then cut across, we should be able to make it to Africa within a year or so." He touched the hand drawn map on the table. "I have a list and a map. What could possibly go wrong?"

"Will it really be different?"

"Well, the last trader that came through said people are headin' that way. He said he even saw an airplane once. If there's airplanes, there's cities, and if there's cities, there's food."

Joey sat up stiffly. "An airplane? A real one? Flying?"

"That's what the man said."

"Wow! A real airplane." He had spent many hours at the deserted airport on the edge of town examining frozen skeletons of abandoned planes. They had been stripped of everything usable, but he often sat for hours in a dismantled cockpit surveying the carcasses of the other planes and imagining what they were like before. He'd pretend he was flying, and the snow covered runways were bustling with people and strange, mechanized vehicles like the pictures in Mother's books.

Thinking about airplanes brought back his excitement about tomorrow. The toes of his boots began tapping against the floor, and wiggly things did somersaults in his stomach.

Grandpa laughed. "Why don't you go to bed? The other families want to get an early start, and we gotta leave with 'em, 'cause it ain't safe to try that trip alone."

As Joey left the relative warmth of the kitchen and headed to his room, the glaciers groaned again.

Grandpa mumbled something to himself.

Joey barely caught the words, and a dry lump formed in his throat, pushing the thrill of adventure away.

Grandpa sighed. "Yep. They're marching again. Blasted things are gonna' chase us all the way to Africa. Then what?" he asked the doomed empty chair.

Joey glanced back. A single tear glittered like a snowflake, slid slowly down the old man's cheek, found a furrow in his grizzled face and followed it down to disappear in a grey beard. Still sitting at the table, Grandpa looked at the cold, black night outside the kitchen window and sighed softly.

Joey lay awake a long time listening to the ice monoliths growl at each other in the bay. He finally fell asleep and dreamed of a screaming white mountain that chased him across a hot desert filled with people standing in the sand, raising their arms toward Heaven.

BIO: S. Joan Popek was owner and editor of *Millennium Science Fiction & Fantasy Magazine* and *The Roswell Literary Review.* She also wrote a monthly column called *Ask Dr. WEB-Write* for Millennium.

She has been published in over 250 fiction, nonfiction and poetry works in various magazines. Her books, *The Administrator, Sound The Ram's Horn,* and *Fairy Tales With A Freudian Flair* are available from Amazon. *The Administrator* won the 2000 EPPIE Award, and her nonfiction book, *Jumpstart Your Career With Electronic Publishing,* was a 2002 EPPIE Finalist.

The Blind Date

by Regina Puckett
Award Winning Guest Author

"I have a list and a map. What could possibly go wrong?" Tiffany tucked a short, auburn curl behind her ear while her best friend examined the map in question.

Barbara all but threw it back at her before sniggering. "So let me get this straight. Your blind date sent you a map drawn in red, yellow and green crayons, and his list tells you to bring a chocolate candy bar, orange soda and a puppy? Really? Is your blind date three years old?"

Tiffany stuffed the list and map into her purse. "Of course not. Beverly says he has big blue eyes and is adorable."

"Adorable? Babies and pets are adorable. Men are handsome and sexy. If I were you, I would call and tell this guy you can't come because you need to wash your hair, or better still, you have scurvy." She rolled her eyes and giggled. "Does anyone actually get scurvy these days?"

Tiffany shrugged. "I've already promised Beverly I would meet her brother. What's the worst thing that can possibly happen tonight? I'm driving my own car to the restaurant so I can leave any time I want, so what if the guy is into candy and puppies? I happen to like candy and puppies, too." She held up a hand to forestall any further argument. "I'll call you in the morning to give you all the juicy details."

The unskillfully drawn map and instructions took Tiffany directly to a cute fifties style hamburger joint, complete with carhops on roller-skates. Resisting the urge to take her soda, candy and stuffed puppy and hightail it back to the safety of her apartment, she opened the car door and hurried in before she changed her mind. Beverly's description of Anthony McBride had been a tad sketchy. Blonde, blue eyes and red sneakers weren't much to go on, but she scanned the crowded restaurant all the same.

The sounds of giggling caught her attention, and when she looked across at the corner booth from whence it came, she couldn't believe its occupant could possibly be her date. A little reluctantly, she went on over.

"Anthony?"

A pair of huge, beautiful blue eyes turned in her direction and the sweetest smile ever filled his face when he said, "Uh huh."

Tiffany held out the bag holding the requested items. When he took it, she asked, "Do you mind if I join you?"

He was too busy admiring the stuffed dog to look up, but he nodded, so she took that as an invitation. She slid into the booth opposite him, intrigued to see what the rest of her blind date held in store. She had known right up front it was going to be an odd one because the entire time Beverly had been trying to talk her into going out with her brother, she didn't stop laughing. Tiffany only agreed because she'd not wanted to hurt her feelings. So here she was, sitting across from a child who couldn't have been much older than four.

Feeling as if someone were watching, she looked over his shoulder and found an extremely handsome, older version of Anthony sitting in the next booth. When their eyes met, he grinned and mouthed, "Sorry."

His expression was so sincere Tiffany relaxed immediately. She returned his grin, but then had to smother a giggle when he held up a menu and some cash. Clearly, dinner was on him. Was *he* Beverly's brother? Tiffany really hoped so because, as cute as the young man sitting in front of her was, the older version was drop-dead, let's-meet-your-parents gorgeous.

It took some doing, but she finally broke eye contact with Mr. Gorgeous and she looked at the young boy across the table. "Do you have a name picked out for your new puppy?"

Anthony sat the red, floppy-eared hound next to him and gave her his full attention. A deep dimple marred his otherwise serious expression. "Catsup."

Tiffany had been so busy trying to figure out what was going on, she had lost track of the question he was answering. "Catsup?" she said.

He nodded and grinned, revealing a huge gap between his front teeth. "My puppy. His name is Catsup."

"Catsup's a good name." She pulled his map

out of her purse. "Thanks to your map, I didn't have any trouble at all finding this place."

"Aunt Beverly helped me. She drew it, but I colored it." He picked up Catsup and hugged the stuffed dog to his chest. His big blue eyes peered over the top of its head, as if unsure what to do now that she was here.

Her good friend Beverly would have a lot of explaining to do when they met up for their Friday girl's-night-out.

Anthony sat Catsup on the tabletop and pulled over the candy bar. He held it in midair. "Dad won't let me eat candy before dinner, but I like chocolate."

Tiffany made eye contact with Anthony's father. He was clearly amused at how she was going to handle the candy-before-dinner thing, so she stifled a giggle. "I love chocolate, too, but I would always want to have my hamburger before eating my dessert, but then, this is your dinner date, so why don't you decide?"

Anthony drew his legs up under him so he could sit on his knees in the seat. He leaned across the table, his whisper embarrassingly loud, "You're so pretty. Would you like to be my mommy?"

Tiffany heard strangled chuckles coming from the next booth but dared not look at Anthony's father. She was going to kill Beverly the next time she saw her. What could she say that wouldn't break this kid's heart?

She leaned forward, speaking as low as the loud restaurant would allow. "Shouldn't your father be the one to find you a new mommy? What if you bring me home and he doesn't like me?"

"But you're beautiful," and he held up his new puppy, "and you knew I would love Catsup." Big tears filled his eyes. "Please?"

When his bottom lip quivered, her heart broke at the sight. Now totally at a loss, she sent a silent plea to Anthony's father and was greatly relieved when he slid in next to his son.

Once settled, he focused all his attention on Tiffany. "Anthony McBride, but it might be less confusing to just call me Tony." He held out his hand and added, "I'm your blind date's father."

Tiffany accepted his hand, but instead of a handshake, Tony lifted her fingers to his lips and gently kissed them. It was such an old-fashioned gesture that it sent a jolt of electricity all the way to her toes. Oh my. She was in trouble with this guy. But then it struck her how he was unfairly using his son to charm women into going out with him, and so slipped her hand free and kept her tone formal.

"It's nice meeting you, but..."

"But?" and the smile on his face slipped.

She looked at his adorable son, uncertain how to broach her misgivings.

He must have sensed it. "Anthony, see if you can get a waitress to come over." As soon as the boy slipped out of the booth, Tony said, "I know how this must look, but believe me, I had no idea Anthony and Beverly had cooked up a blind date until forty-five minutes ago. By then it was too late to call it off. I would really appreciate it if you would just play along for a little while. Anthony has his heart set on finding a new mother. All the kids in his daycare class have theirs, and lately it has left him feeling as though he's missing out on something."

She opened her mouth to speak but he held up his hand. "Please. I'll figure out a way to end the date without putting you on the spot again." He looked across the room at his son and smiled. "He has a heart of gold, but he's too young to understand that he can't go around begging beautiful women to be his mother."

Why not? Both father and son were charming, and she was getting a free meal with the deal. "So, do you think I'm beautiful?"

He met her eyes again and laughed. "Oh, yeah."

She was such a sucker for big blue eyes. "Okay, but Anthony and I get to eat our desserts first. Right? He kind of has his heart set on it, and I think he should have at least one thing go right for him on this blind date."

Anthony was almost back with a waitress, so Tiffany leaned forward and whispered, "Deal?"

They shook hands seconds before Anthony climbed back over his father's lap and settled down with Catsup in his own.

Tiffany tapped a finger on the candy bar. "Plans have changed. We're eating dessert before ordering dinner."

Anthony squealed, "Really? Dad?"

Tony turned to the waitress. "Orange sodas all

around."

As soon as they'd consumed the candy and sodas, all three ordered hamburgers and fries. It didn't surprise them that, having already eaten the candy, Anthony only pushed his food around on his plate. It also didn't take him long to become bored with grownup conversation so his eyes were soon drooping.

With Anthony nodding off against Tony, the two adults chatted on until she finally leaned forward and whispered, "I think my date has fallen asleep. Maybe you should take him home now."

Tony glanced down at his son. "I think you're right, but I'd hate to leave without him saying goodbye. Plus, when he wakes up in the morning, he's going to be real upset that you never answered his question."

Tiffany grabbed a couple of clean napkins from the holder and a pen out of her purse. She scribbled away, and after a moment, handed Tony two notes.

He quirked an eyebrow. "A map and a list?"

She chuckled and nodded. "The map will get you and Anthony to the park next to my apartment building, and the list is self-explanatory."

"Daisies, ice cream and hot dogs?" He folded the napkins and tucked them into his shirt pocket.

"Daisies are my favorite flowers. I love chocolate ice cream, and the hot dogs are for a picnic in the park. If I'm going to give any thought to being your son's mother, I think we're going to need a second date, at the very least."

Anthony stirred but didn't wake when Tony said, "Thank you."

"For what?"

He reached over and took her hand. "For not breaking my son's heart."

She squeezed his fingers. "How could I? He's very sweet, and I suspect his father is, too." She sat back. "So what do you say to another date?"

Tony patted his pocket. "I have a list and a map. What could possibly go wrong?"

BIO: Regina Puckett writes sweet romances, horror, inspirational, picture books and poetry. There are several projects in various stages of completion and there are always characters and stories waiting for their chance to finally get out of her head and onto paper.

Three Kinds of Kisses

by Jan Romes
Award Winning Guest Author

Libby James walked the last row of the Christmas tree farm searching for just the right tree while braving a slippery mix of rain and snow. The lucky tree wouldn't have to be the tallest or fullest, but it had to have character. From the corner of her eye, she homed in on a sparse Douglas-fir with a few broken limbs. Traipsing to the misfit evergreen, she tried to imagine it decked out with energy-saving lights, brightly colored ornaments, and tinsel.

A friendly male voice sounded behind her. "Can I help you?"

"Yes. I think I've found the one I want." Libby turned and met an amazing set of blue eyes. Her stomach did a weird flip. *Hmm!* That hadn't happened before.

The ruggedly handsome man, with a sexy five o'clock shadow, pulled the tree upright so she could inspect it. He pointed to an obvious crook in the trunk.

Libby studied the flaw and drew the conclusion that with a little love and creativity, the tree could still sparkle and fill her apartment with the scent of pine.

"Sorry, Ma'am, I can't sell this tree."

Libby's attention zipped back to the hunky

salesman and, all at once, she wished she didn't look so frumpy. Her long, blonde hair smashed beneath a polyester Trooper hat with ear flaps, and her jeans had holes in the knees. It was freezing outside, so the hat was a good choice, and she didn't want to haul a sappy pine home in good clothes. "Why not?" she said.

Shaking his head, the man apologized again. "Sorry. Mel takes pride in selling the best Christmas trees around." The corners of his mouth pulled into a smile. "The *best* is subjective I guess. Between you and me, the tree has personality." He winked. "If I want to keep my job, I'd better talk you into a different one."

Libby hawk-eyed his nametag. "Garrett." She modestly cleared her throat. "The tree might be scraggly, but to me it's perfect."

Garrett appeared to mull over the comment. "Not-so-perfect is sometimes-perfect?"

"Exactly." Libby was confused by the unexpected warm, fuzzy feeling.

"I didn't catch your name." The rough gravel of his voice switched her warm-fuzzy to tingles of excitement.

"It's Libby." Her heart began to thud louder than the crunch of snow beneath her feet.

"Nice to meet you, Libby."

"Nice to meet you, Garrett."

The wintry mix of precipitation changed to stinging pellets of ice.

Garrett pointed to a log cabin gift shop beyond the rows of trees. "Care for a cup of coffee while we wait for Mother Nature to come to her senses?"

"Sounds great." A few steps into the trek, Libby's feet slid out from under her. Before face-planting on the frozen ground, she was caught by a pair of strong arms.

Garrett kept both of them from falling by bringing them chest to chest. Heartbeat to heartbeat. Blush to blush.

"Thank you," Libby said, breathlessly.

For a long moment, neither blinked.

Garrett finally smiled. "No problem." He took her hand and slowly led the way down a slick path.

They made it to the rustic gift shop without wiping out or breaking bones. Libby stepped inside and was met by the heavenly smell of cinnamon and hazelnut. "If the coffee tastes as good as it smells, I might need two cups."

Garrett grinned and hung their coats. He gestured at a plate of sugar cookies sitting on the counter. "Help yourself," he said, and then pointed to shelves along the wall. "I'm supposed to tell you about the pine cone wreaths, hand-poured candles, and beaded ornaments." On his way to the back room, he wiggled his eyebrows up and down. "And we also have mistletoe."

Libby's cheeks burned. When Garrett was out of sight, she inspected the mistletoe. There were three ways to press one's lips against another: soft pecks on the cheek for friendship, light lip-to-lip action for casual dating, and a full-mouth-extravaganza for that special person you wanted to kiss for the rest of your life. So far, she'd experienced the first two.

She checked out the scented candles. There was cranberry-orange, peppermint-pine, ginger-clove, and vanilla bean. Libby removed the lid on the peppermint-pine, closed her eyes, and took a whiff. The essence of Christmas had been captured. Opening her eyes, she looked the candle over. A sticker on the bottom of the jar caught her attention. It read: *Never Give Up! All proceeds go to those fighting cancer.* Libby's heart clenched and wondered if someone close to Mel or Garrett had fought the dreaded battle. She prayed they had won.

The sound of boots on rough-hewn floorboards made Libby turn. She held up the candle. "I'll take three of these."

"Excellent. My no-pressure technique worked." Garrett smiled and handed her a steamy cup of coffee.

She searched his eyes for a clue about the message on the bottom of the candles. The only thing she saw was a sexy sparkle that messed with her equilibrium. Diverting her gaze for a second, she braved another look at those deep-blue orbs and caught Garrett doing the same to her. Their eyes held for an overly long moment. To distract the blush creeping into her cheeks, she took a sip of coffee. "Ohhhh, that's good."

Garrett mimicked her with a sip. He smacked his lips. "Mighty fine." He motioned for her to have a seat.

Libby perched on a brocade-padded stool and

tucked her feet behind the rungs while Garrett leaned against the counter.

The next twenty minutes were heaven. She discovered how easy it was to talk with him. It was as if they'd known each other forever. They talked about football and dogs. Garrett had a cocker spaniel named Roy. Libby was owned by a Siberian husky affectionately known as Jax. They had similar addictions – coffee and the television show, *NCIS*.

The owner of the tree farm and gift shop poked her head around the door. "The roads are getting nasty. I don't want to shoo you away, but it might be a good idea to leave while there's daylight." Melanie Thompson, also known as Mel, motioned to Garrett. "There's a car in the ditch a mile down the road. They could use your help. Use the log chain in the back of the pickup."

Garrett rang up her candle purchase. "Duty calls. It was great meeting you, Libby." He hesitated, as though he wanted to say more. Instead, he helped with her coat and took her hand. "I'll make sure you get to your truck without falling on your keister."

"Thank you."

Garrett made sure she was tucked safely inside her car, smiled as he closed the door, and plodded toward Mel's truck. Looking over his shoulder, he smiled and waved. When he continued on, Libby noticed a small hitch in his walk. She glanced at the sack setting on the passenger seat and remembered the sticker on the bottom of the jars. Hmm.

Over the next forty-eight hours, snow and high winds consumed the county. A snow emergency had been declared with only plows, police, ambulance, and utility repair vehicles permitted on the roadways.

Garrett stayed inside until he thought he'd go crazy. Finally, he started plowing driveways as he thought about Libby. There was something enchanting about the brown-eyed blonde. He pictured her in that adorable Trooper hat and those torn jeans, wishing he'd asked for her phone number.

After plowing the drive at the last house, which belonged to his friend, Len Greenwood, he was invited in to get warm. The second he stepped inside, the smell of cinnamon-hazelnut met his nose. Was it a poke of divine intervention? Garrett couldn't deny there had been an attraction between them. What would she think if he showed up at her door? More importantly, how would she react when she discovered his physical limitations?

"Len, I've got a question. Actually, I have two."

Over a second cup of coffee, he talked about Libby and his uncertainty about trying to find her.

"What do you have to lose?" Len said.

Garrett rubbed his hand along his hip. "What if …"

Len shook his head. "Don't even go there. Any woman worth her salt will love you exactly as you are." Len placed a hand on Garrett's shoulder. "What are you waiting for?"

Garrett smiled and took off like his feet were on fire. Before he got to his truck, he drew to a halt and retraced his steps back to Len.

In the meantime, Libby paced from window to window. In the rush to get home before the storm, she hadn't bargained for the perfect, albeit spindly, tree. Christmas was only a week away and she still had no tree with twinkling lights to put her in the holiday spirit. The weather had interfered – in more ways than one. She'd also forgotten to ask Garrett's last name, nor had she offered hers. Maybe she'd stop by after Christmas and buy more candles. She shook her head. She wasn't one to chase men, no matter how dreamy. Was he the guy she'd always pined for? Christmas tree. Pine. She giggled.

She spied her stack of CD's and popped *All I Want for Christmas Is You* by Mariah Carey into the CD player. Singing and dancing to the music, she strung strands of twinkle lights around the windows. Soft hands smoothed a linen tablecloth decorated with holly and arranged resin snowmen on a hallway table. Last, but not least, lit candles in a log centerpiece offered tranquility. Hitting the replay button one more time, Libby looked in the mirror. If she had one wish this Christmas…

A sudden knock at the door made her jerk.

Peering through the peek-hole, a smile of recognition met her face. She whipped the door open and tried to contain her excitement, although her heart was thudding in her chest. "Garrett?"

"You left without a tree." Her eyes turned to the scraggly pine she'd fallen in love with.

Libby's mouth dropped open. "You brought

my tree?"

"And something else." Garrett pulled a sprig of mistletoe from his coat pocket. "It'll give us something to do between cups of coffee and decorating this little fellow."

Libby hugged him. A blustery blast of wind made her shiver. She pulled him, tree and all, inside. "How'd you get here?"

"My tractor." He put a finger to his lips. "I'm not supposed to be out and about."

Libby wanted to squeal with joy. "How did you find me? I mean, you don't even know my last name. It's James, by the way."

Garrett laughed. "I have a list and a map. What could possibly go wrong?"

Libby was confused. "What kind of list?"

"My friend and I went through the phone book looking for anyone named Libby. We found two. I circled the addresses on the map."

"You went to a lot of trouble."

Garrett held up the mistletoe with a grin.

Libby impulsively pecked his cheek. "There are three kinds of kisses. One down. Two to go."

Garrett smiled with his eyes. "Before we get to the other two, there's something you should know."

"What is it?"

Garrett shifted from foot to foot. "It's hard to point out your flaws to the person you're attracted to."

Libby lifted the cranberry orange candle and turned it over. "All proceeds go to those fighting cancer."

"I had a tumor on my hip joint. It was the scare of a lifetime. Thankfully, it was benign. After I healed, Mel and I decided to help those whose diagnosis wasn't so fortunate."

"That's such a loving thing to do, Garrett." Libby moved closer. "You don't have to be absolutely perfect… for me." She wet her lips, eager to engage in the full-mouth-extravaganza she'd saved for that special person she wanted to kiss for the rest of her life.

BIO: Jan Romes is a hopeless romantic who grew up in Ohio with eight zany siblings. Married to her high school sweetheart for more years than seems possible, she is also a proud mom, mother-in-law, and grandmother. She likes to read all genres, writes witty contemporary romance, and enjoys growing pumpkins and sunflowers.

A Rum Tale

by Iain Pattison
2013 Short Story 1st Place Winner

A sudden lewd cackle made him jump. Scanning the teeming twilight-bathed dock, Sly Jake immediately saw the source of the licentious laughter and broke into an envious smile. A drunken sailor was clumsily groping a giggling harlot, both swaying like square-riggers in a gale, narrowly avoiding being mowed down by a thundering cart speeding over the cobbles.

Spinning around, Jake saw the whole waterfront was packed with similar scenes. Mariners and trollops, all inebriated beyond reason, all barely able to stand. Three ships of the line had moored that afternoon and their crews - deprived of grog, girls and decent grub for months - were making up for lost time.

Grinning, he scratched his unshaven cheek with the iron hook where his right hand used to be. He knew sozzled sailors were a soft touch, always ready to stand a drink for a friendly, ingratiating stranger, and Jake hadn't tasted spirits in days. Not since he'd gambled away his last piece-of-eight at poker - discovering that it was possible for your opponent to win with five aces if he had a unique interpretation of the rules, a loaded blunderbuss and the meanest accomplices in the Caribbean.

Jake swallowed hard at the memory and the dryness in his throat. He desperately needed a drop of rum. So, there was only one solution - find a gullible audience.

But which inn? He hadn't been thrown out of The Admiral Jericho for a while, and it was just around the corner.

The sawdust-floored tavern was so packed that Jake had to shove his way through the heaving, hedonistic humanity. The smells of roast pork, stale ale, pipe smoke and urine assailed his nostrils. Jack Tars from HMS Respite had taken over the place. They filled every corner, every nook, lounging on upturned barrels where there were no chairs, laughing, singing, cursing and arguing. The racket was deafening.

Looking over to the bar, he recognized the ship's bosun, uniform askew, balding head buried deep in barmaid Betsy's generous cleavage. The three pink domes bobbed like buoys in a swell, making it difficult to tell where the bosun ended and bosoms began.

"Hey, me lads, listen up," Jake said, fighting to be heard over the din. "This be yer lucky night."

No one paid any attention.

"Boys, be quiet and lend me your ear," he said, speaking louder. "I've got a rollockin' delight in store for ye."

If anyone heard, they gave no sign. Jake grabbed an empty pewter flagon from a nearby table and brought it crashing down as hard as he could.

ONCE

TWICE
THREE TIMES

All eyes swiveled to stare, curious at who had disturbed the revels, and doing little to hide their seething annoyance.

He cleared his throat. "Shipmates, good friends, fellow seadogs, let me introduce myself. I be Captain Jake Pritheroe - former privateer and pirate - known to most as Sly Jake. At your service." He bowed theatrically.

"For twenty and five long years, I've sailed these here high seas, voyaged to exotic lands, survived hair-raising adventures and seen ungodly sights ye'd not believe in your wildest nightmares. And for a small libation, I'll recount one of my most terrifying adventures - a story to chill your vitals; a cautionary tale of fiendish forces, dark doings and drooling hell-fire creatures of the night. What say ye, lads?"

A grizzled man in an eye patch leaned forward and spat noisily. "I'd say we should cut your tongue out and be done with it," he hissed. "We've all heard your fancy fools' tales before, Lying Jake."

"That's right," a voice rang out. "Like the one where you had a night of passion with a mermaid …"

The revelers sniggered.

"Or the time you sailed to the land where the inhabitants were just eight inches high."

"Yeah, and the unforgettable occasion when you were turned into a goat by a sea witch."

The teasing mirth had a nasty undertone.

Drawing in his breath, Jake studied the room. It could go either way.

"All righty, all righty, mates. Maybe, perchance, I have… *sometimes*… let me imagination run a little wild before the trade winds," he conceded. "I may have exaggerated a teensy detail here and there, but I ain't never set out to deceive. And tonight, I promise ye, I'll be telling this esteemed gathering the God's honest truth."

He looked beseechingly at the barmaid. "All I ask is a flagon of ale and a tot of rum to wash it down and I'll tell ye how I lost this …" He waved his hook above his head. "… to a monstrous, howling demon from the bowels of Hades itself!"

The balding bosun groaned loudly, but Jake knew he'd succeeded. The audience was curious. They leaned forward, aghast.

Signaling Betsy to give the storytelling seadog what he'd asked for, Eye Patch told Jake to get on with it. "But this better be good, you old twister, or I promise you'll lose the other hand."

Slurping down the welcome beer and letting it slosh against his throat, Jake made his voice soft and deep, with just the right edge of menace.

"It all happened on an eerie evening just like this," he began slowly, motioning them to draw close. "There was a ghostly galleon moon high in the heavens, and we'd been at sea for five, interminable, tormented, soul-sapping months …"

* * *

Five…

Interminable…
Tormented…
Soul-sapping…
Months…

Jake was surprised it had taken The Crooked Contessa's hapless pirate band that long to start grumbling and demand to go home. A ragbag collection of old men, rejects from other ships, wide-eyed shop boys, simpletons, braggarts and drunks, the Contessa's crew were, he conceded, not so much a complement as a calculated insult. Only two factors united them - their seasickness and their cowardice, an alliance of yellow spines and churning stomachs.

"C'mon lads, we can't turn back now," Jake said when they assembled outside his cabin. "The ship is barely out of sight of port. Where's ye sense of adventure?"

"Back on the dockside," Tom, the cabin boy replied, to nods from the rest of the bedraggled delegation.

"And we wants to make its acquaintance again as soon as possible," the ship's one-legged cook agreed, leaning on the wooden crutch that kept him vertical. "Turn around, Captain. Take us home. No good can come of this foolishness."

Foolishness? Getting their filthy hands on enough booty to last a lifetime? Plundering and carousing their way into the history books? Staying up past midnight and singing shanties with rude words?

"We're pleading with ye," young Tom added, with an apologetic shrug.

Jake curled his lip. They were a load of pleaders, all right. He promised himself that one day he'd make them walk the plank - if he ever got around to buying one.

For now, however, he had an idea. "Tell you what, boys. I can tell yer obviously not up for a cruise, so why don't we head back to land …"

The company cheered.

"… and see if we can slip past Mad Morgan's hound and pinch all his loot."

The company groaned. They stepped back one pace, shaking their heads in trembling protest.

Every man had heard the rumors - that Morgan, the most feared privateer on the entire Spanish Main, had a dog even more barking than him, even more bloodcurdling, aggressive and ugly than his crossed-eyed, tobacco-chewing, cannon-fisted wife. It was said to guard the caves at the foot of Smashed Skull cliffs… caves that were used as the depository for Morgan's trove of tantalizing treasure.

Many had tried to steal the riches, but none had succeeded. Chillingly, not a single man had ever returned to say why.

"Look, it's just a dog," Jake said, bringing both hands closer together to help conjure an image of a small, endearing terrier.

The crew wasn't having it. They spread their hands at arm's length, conjuring up a picture of a large, snarling, entrails-ripping terror.

Jake sighed. There was nothing for it. He'd have to rely on his charisma and charm to win them.

Two minutes later, his charisma had predictably failed, but the charm proved a winner. It should be, he reminded himself, it was the most powerful and expensive hex he'd ever stolen.

Swigging from a bottle of brandy, and noting that he was keeling over alarmingly from its brain-numbing effects, he beamed at the spell-bound crew and waved the yellowing parchment that revealed the location of the swag.

"I have a list and a map. What can possibly go wrong?" he said.

* * *

The oars clattered wildly, sending up volley after volley of splashes as the longboat made its haphazard way through the swirling, spectral mist. With each chaotic stroke, the boat threatened to tip, going 'round in dizzying circles. Jake marveled at how inept his sidekicks could be at even this simple seafaring task.

"Pull together," he hissed, miming the action the clueless cutthroats should be taking. "Both paddles going the same way!"

Then, with a sudden crunch and a collective yelp of surprise, they made contact with terra firma, scraping the jagged rocks guarding the beach, and Jake found himself flying through the air before making landfall with a jarring thud.

"Everyone all right?" he asked the tangled mass of arms and legs that sprawled across the wet sand.

Groans, curses, a cry of "I want my mother," and three vehemently expressed offers of resignation came hurtling back.

"Any broken bones?" he enquired.

"Not yet," a deep, murderous voice replied.

Sighing, Jake got to his feet, dusted himself off and signaled his crumpled companions to follow.

"C'mon shipmates. Don't be down at heart. It'll be a dawdle from here on in. Look up yonder… Smashed Skull's caves and the treasure just waiting for us."

At that very moment, a nerve-jangling, primal, bowel-loosening howl rent the night air. The crew immediately concluded a hoard of doubloons wasn't the only thing waiting for them. For injured men, they got to their feet in an impressive surge of motion, sprinting back toward the longboat.

It was an ironic switch of events. Normally, a gunshot begins a race. On this occasion, it stopped them dead in their tracks.

"And I've still got another flintlock," Jake informed his minions as they froze and looked around, warily.

He waved the musket toward their destination. "Come about, me hearties. The caves are that way."

* * *

One after another, each man's mouth fell open, revealing their surprise and the fact that the noble science of dentistry hadn't yet made it to the Spice Isles. They leaned forward as one, curiosity overcoming their natural fearfulness.

Yards away, silhouetted against the dancing flames of the tar-dipped torches hanging from the dank, moldy walls of the mountain entrance, a sight greeted them that left all trembling and bewildered.

"Yon can't be a dog," cabin boy Tom murmured in awe. "It's too large."

"And too tall," the beer-bellied buccaneer next to him agreed.

As if sensing that it was being talked about, the giant feral vision turned blazing crimson eyes toward them and snarled, sniffing the air hungrily.

Jake gulped. The lads were right. This was no mere mutt. The burly beast wasn't covered in hair, but gleaming fur. It was a wolf, and a particularly mean looking specimen. He had seen plenty of the deadly predators before, and this one easily dwarfed them.

Staring transfixed at the drooling, rumbling creature, two questions nagged at him. What was a wolf doing in these alien, tropical parts? He had only encountered them on voyages to the chilly lands up north, and even then, only in deep woodlands. And even more puzzling, why was it standing on two legs instead of four?

For a full minute, Jake's brain refused to accept the obvious, and then he let his gaze rise to the dazzling white orb hanging high in the night sky, the wide full disc. Not just a wolf then… but something much worse. An abomination that shouldn't exist outside of legend.

He frowned. Part of his brain said seizing Mad

Morgan's pension pot was suicide, but the other part, where greed lurked, whispered seductive words. *You outnumber the monster twenty to one.* "Okay, lads. On the count of three, we're going to charge it," he whispered down the line.

He couldn't tell which scurvy cur replied cheekily, "How much?" and didn't have the opportunity to find out, for at that instant, the beast took matters into his own paws and, bellowing loud enough to shake the trees, surged forward, covering the ground in supernaturally long strides. There wasn't time to flee before it was upon them.

It should have been a battle to go down in the annals of bandit lore, a derring-do action guaranteed to inspire a dozen rousing, boozy ballads, but as the creature tore its way through the sobbing, saber-waving rabble, the muddled melee quickly descended into a rout.

Savage snarls mixed with screams as the men went down one by one. It ripped through them like rag dolls, crunching bones, tearing out throats and hurling lifeless bodies over its shoulder.

Jake had often been asked if he had a pirate's chest, and at that moment, his madly thumping heart nearly burst clean through it. He stood frozen, paralyzed in fear, raised his flintlock and took careful aim. The gun thundered, sending a searing metal sphere through the air, seeking its target with a deadly sizzle and murderous intent. It made solid contact, but to Jake's astonishment, it bounced harmlessly off the wolf-man's rock-hard pelt. At that instant, he knew he was booked on a one-way trip to Davy Jones' locker.

He'd heard that when facing death, a person's whole life flashed in front of his eyes, but very little of the blurry, double vision pictures racing across his pupils seemed familiar. Especially not the episode with the harem girls, the whipped cream and the penguin.

A split second later, he felt sticky fetid breath upon his face and his arm jerked violently as his hand, still holding the weapon, disappeared between the beast's jagged yellow teeth. The jaws snapped shut in one brutal movement, and he felt everything below the wrist detach - bone, flesh and blood parting from the rest of his body in a burst of agony.

Looking up in dismay, he watched the monster gobble down its meaty prize in one gulp, and lick its strangely human lips at the tangy taste. Steeling himself for the inevitable, Jake prayed death would be mercifully quick, but the creature that acted next was a bizarre, hopping dervish.

Out of nowhere, the Contessa's one legged pot-stirrer bounded unsteadily into the fray and, swinging his crutch like a mighty cudgel, walloped the nightmare animal squarely across the skull.

Jake had no idea how the cook had survived the slaughter, but wasn't complaining about the help or the distraction.

"Whack it in the goolies," he said, sharing the experience from a score of bar room brawls.

The cook obliged and the werewolf bellowed in pain and fury as its privates suddenly blazed in torment - much like those who'd had the misfortune of sampling his homebrew asparagus and chili wine.

There was no third blow. As Cookie went to swing the oak prop, the towering brute leapt upon him. Jake guessed it was a desire for symmetry that made the beast yank off the chef's remaining leg. The poor soul's doomed shriek reverberated so loudly that Jake put his hands over his ears, before he remembered the bloody pumping stump wasn't likely to block out any sound.

Then, without warning, the beast froze, startled, in mid gorge. Dropping the mangled leg half eaten, it gave a strangled bark, clawed at its throat, lurched forward, and crashed to the ground lifeless.

* * *

Jake grinned to himself, letting his sly eyes scan the totally enthralled audience, each listener perched on the edge of his seat in excitement and suspense.

"The werewolf was deceased, defunct, departed. Slain in a heartbeat," he whispered dramatically.

"But how?" Eye Patch demanded.

"What killed it?" Betsy asked, agog.

Jake took a final swig of his ale. Not a drop remained. Time to divulge the punch line.

"It were poisoned, having ingested a most deadly substance, the one toxin that could destroy its hellish being," he reported. "For what the monster didn't realize was that our cook was no other than Long …"

He paused for maximum effect –

"… John"

And held his arms out wide –

"… SILVER!"

Lying amongst the fragments of shattered glass moments later, Jake mused that it hadn't gone too badly. At least they hadn't beaten him up before they threw him through the window.

Glancing up at the full moon, he thought it a shame that no one ever believed his shaggy dog stories. Still, that would soon be rectified. The monthly change was already surging through his body, the bestial transformation taking grip. Admiring the fur sprouting from his hook, he calculated that in a few moments he'd banish all doubts.

The rowdy sailors had watered him, but soon it would be time for them to quell his hunger, too. And bosun boy would make such an appetizing starter…

Conflict of Interest

by Christine House
2013 Short Story 2nd Place Winner

Elizabeth waited out Tyler's rant with a poker face. It was a level two tantrum this time so he was running out of steam, which was just as well because she was running out of patience.

"Get on the next flight," he said, pointing a pudgy finger at her chest, "and find out what the devil Jeremy is doing out there!"

Elizabeth walked out of her boss' office and rolled her eyes at the secretary. Everyone at TH Enterprises knew about Tyler's temper, and they all knew how to avoid the consequences, so it was odd that Jeremy hadn't checked in with her or Tyler. She looked at her watch. It was 5:46 p.m., and she was hungry and tired. The last thing she wanted to do was fight rush hour traffic to get on a plane bound for Lyric, Ohio, a place she hadn't been in years. This wouldn't be the homecoming she had planned.

She called for car service and stopped at her condo, kicking off her heels in favor of a comfy pair of boots. The stilettos hurt her feet, but she wore them because Tyler expected his staff to dress up every day. For the women, that meant tight-fitting suits and high-end pumps. No exceptions. "I'm not paying you big bucks so you can buy Birkenstocks," Tyler often said. Elizabeth shoved hangers of clothes into a small suitcase, wondering what Tyler *would* do if she showed up dressed in flats one day. *Not worth the risk,* she thought.

The chauffeur drove aggressively, but it still took an hour to get to the airport. Elizabeth rewarded him with a generous tip, knowing she would hear about it later, but $350 was a small price to pay for losing her weekend. She called Jeremy as she boarded the plane, letting the phone ring several times. Getting no response, she reviewed the text he sent the day he checked into the motel.

Jeremy: The accommodations in your town are below par. A Senior Director deserves better. ☹
Elizabeth: LOL

And that was the last she'd heard from her co-worker. *I should have gone with him*, she thought. They always worked as a team, but Tyler had purposely taken her off the Lyric account. "Conflict of interest," he'd said, and she hadn't protested. After all, her father was listed on the agreement and she knew pretty much everybody in Lyric who had signed over drilling rights to TH Enterprises last year. Now the lease was up for renewal and Jeremy was running lead solo. She remembered the afternoon before he left when she stopped by his office to give him her two cents.

"Don't be too friendly or they'll know you're faking," she said.

"Yes, Ma'am," Jeremy gave a mock salute.

"Trust me, I was born and raised in Lyric. I know what works and what doesn't."

"I'll be just fine."

"Will you?"

"I have a list and a map. What can possibly go wrong?"

As the plane ascended, Elizabeth leaned back in her cramped seat and looked out the small oval window into the wide blackness of the night sky, thinking about all the things that could go wrong in Lyric. The list of names on the lease agreement and the map of the town had been her idea. She had even called her father to give him a heads-up, but he hadn't returned her call. She wondered if it was due to their last conversation at Christmas. Dad had asked where she was spending the holidays. She replied, "With a few friends at the beach." Dad countered with, "Christmas is a family affair," and things went downhill from there. Ever since Mom died and her brother Robbie moved to Texas, her father relentlessly pushed her to move back home. She knew he needed someone to take care of him… but she was just learning how to take care of herself.

"Ladies and gentlemen, this is your captain speaking."

The loud voice on the speaker jolted Elizabeth, and the remains on her Diet Coke spilt onto her lap. She dabbed at the liquid with a tiny napkin but could feel the wetness soaking through her jeans.

"We are about twenty minutes from our destination," the captain continued, "and I just got word that a storm is moving in quickly from the north. At least six inches of snow is expected."

Loud groans erupted in the cabin, but Elizabeth wasn't worried. If there was one thing she'd learned growing up in Lyric, it was how to drive in rain, sleet, snow, and ice. Dad had taught her well. When the flight landed, she picked up her rental car, a sturdy SUV, and hit the road with confidence, but the storm hit when she was a few miles from the motel.

The snow fell so fast that the rental's wipers, even at the fastest setting, could barely keep the windshield clean. It was almost midnight and only a few cars and trucks crept along the highway, including a semi that hauled pigs. The smell was unmistakable. As Elizabeth inched forward with heavy eyelids, the sound of screeching brakes filled the air. Grabbing the wheel hard, she pumped the SUV's brakes to avoid spinning vehicles that skidded left and right to avoid the jack-knifed trailer, but there was no stopping. She veered into the ditch on the side of the road.

When she finally came to, her lips were swelling, thanks to the exploded air bag. Feeling nothing more than a few bruises, she opened the car door and stepped into three feet of snow. Later, as she peeled off her boots in the dingy motel room, she marveled that her feet had somehow remained dry throughout the entire escapade. No way could she have pulled that off in high heels.

As she sank into the lumpy mattress and stared at the patched ceiling, Elizabeth puzzled over the conversations she'd had that evening. After the pile-up, the wind and snow intensified, and the highway patrol had a heck of a time getting people and pigs off the road. Her SUV was buried up to the axle, so she rode in the police van with Ray, a scrawny man whose red pick-up truck also ended up in the ditch, and Officer Peters, the cop assigned to drop-off duty.

"What's your destination, Ma'am?" Peters said, raising his eyebrows at Elizabeth.

"I'm staying at the motel off Route 18," she said, "but I'm on my way home to Lyric." She felt an urge to explain why she wasn't staying *in* Lyric, but held her tongue. Her family drama was none of Officer Peters' business.

"I didn't see the Lyric PD out there tonight," she added. "Not their jurisdiction?"

"Well, the call went out to everyone," Peters shrugged.

Scrawny Ray cleared his throat. "You know, I ain't seen nobody from Lyric lately. My boy, Jonesy, lives out there and I been calling him, but he don't pick up. I stopped by to visit last week. Drove through town, and it was empty as a bucket with a hole in it. Never seen it like that before."

Peters snorted and waved his hand dismissively.

"Anyway, Jonesy wouldn't open the door. I know he was in there 'cos I heard him moving around. Sounded like a dog was in there with him, too, but I ain't never known Jonesy to keep pets," Ray said through a crooked smile.

Elizabeth said nothing, but she could tell Ray was worried about the lad. No more was said about Jonesy, and Ray disembarked a few minutes later. The next stop was the motel.

"Need help with your bags, Ma'am?" Peters said.

"No, thank you," Elizabeth said. "When do you think I'll get my car back?"

Peters shrugged again and swung the door shut. *Not much of a talker*, Elizabeth thought as she rolled her mini suitcase into the empty lobby. She pushed the bell at the check-in desk, waiting for what seemed like an eternity before a short, disheveled man appeared.

"Help you?" the man said, rubbing sleep out of his eyes.

"Checking in," she said, handing over her ID and credit card.

The man didn't bother to look up her reservation. He swiped the credit card and handed her a plastic key.

"Room 12. Around back, first door on the left."

"Thank you. Wait, I have a question."

The clerk, halfway into the office, turned around and yawned.

"I'd like to leave a message for a guest," Elizabeth said. "His name is Jeremy Black."

"Tall guy, kinda skinny?"

"Yeah, that's him."

"Haven't seen him since Tuesday morning," the clerk said, turning away.

"He hasn't been back since Tuesday?" Elizabeth repeated, moving around the desk. She peered into the dark office.

"That's what I said, ain't it? Anyway, I'm not supposed to give out information about the guests. You a cop?" The clerk gave her a suspicious once-over.

"No, I work with him and…"

"Like I said, he ain't been back since Tuesday. You see him, you tell him we charge 'til check out." With that, the clerk closed the door, leaving Elizabeth standing alone in the lobby under flickering fluorescent lights.

She retreated to her room and called Jeremy again. No answer. Next, she tried her father. No answer. Elizabeth slammed the phone into the cradle and then, of course, it rang. Her pulse quickened as she looked at the caller ID – unknown number. She held her breath and answered, but it was just the owner of the towing company. He would drop the SUV off the following afternoon. *Tomorrow I'll find out why Jeremy and Dad are MIA,* she thought, drifting off into a fitful sleep.

It turned out Scrawny Ray was right. Elizabeth didn't see a single soul in Lyric as she drove down Main Street. Eerie, especially for Saturday. She considered stopping at the police station but decided to go home first. Dad would know what was going on. The house she grew up in was only a few miles outside of town.

The driveway was covered in white drifts of snow and Elizabeth was surprised her father hadn't cleared it yet. She abandoned the SUV again, and walked to the front door, which stood wide open.

The porch looked rundown and shabby.

"Dad? You home?" Elizabeth called, stomping snow off her boots.

The only response was a thick silence. She shivered, feeling silly as goose bumps crawled up her arms, then stepped into the parlor. The room was only used for company and the furniture still sat in the plastic covering it arrived in years ago. With the blinds drawn, it took a moment for her eyes to adjust, and when she finally spotted him, she wasn't sure what she was seeing was real. Jeremy lay sprawled on the settee, his head at an obscene angle, his throat torn to shreds. Blood had pooled and dried on the wooden floorboards, forming a large, inky stain. Flies perched on his eyes.

Elizabeth opened her mouth to scream but no sound came out. Something shuffled behind her and she whipped around, almost tripping over her feet. Someone was on the stairs, standing in the shadows.

"Dad? Is that you?"

"Lizzie. I knew you'd come."

Her father's voice sounded strange, but she couldn't put her finger on what was so different. She inched a little closer to the stairwell, trying to make out his face.

"Dad?"

"Yes, Lizzie?"

"I've been calling you all week," Elizabeth said, her own voice shaking. "Where have you been?"

The steps creaked as the shadowy form descended in jerky motion, very unlike his usual purposeful movements. Elizabeth squinted at the obscure shape. Her instincts screamed *RUN*, but loyalty told her to stay.

As if reading her mind, the shadow croaked, "I'm sorry, Lizzie. He was trespassing."

Jeremy? Trespassing? A cold sweat trickled down Elizabeth's back.

"Dad, Jeremy didn't mean any harm. He was…"

"It's the water, Lizzie. Because of the drilling. It's in the water, and I can't help myself. I get so… so *thirsty*."

"Dad, what are you talking about?"

The shadow lurched forward but remained out of focus. The atmosphere was turgid and Elizabeth pushed the front door back for fresh air. She could barely make out her father's brown overalls in the late afternoon light. When she was a kid, she called the overalls his "uniform" because he wore them day in and day out. He'd never seemed to mind. It had been their private joke. Her gaze moved up the legs, resting on her father's hands. The nails were long and sharp like eagle's talons.

"Dad, what's going on?"

It happened quickly. The shadow jumped down the stairs, landed in front of her, and Elizabeth stifled another scream when she saw a wrinkled, pallid mask of a face with black eyes sunk deep in the sockets. His hair had been replaced by a shiny, bald dome, and his mouth was a wide, red scar. And the teeth… dear God, the teeth…

Elizabeth stumbled and fell backwards onto

the dusty porch. The thing came after her, but stopped short at the stoop, shying away from the fading afternoon light. He stood there, growling at her like a rabid dog, spittle flying down his chin. She picked herself up, ignoring the splinters in her palms, and raced to the car. When she looked back, he was still at the door, watching her, his teeth bared like a hungry wolf. She didn't remember clambering into the SUV or sliding out of the snowy driveway. She drove much too fast down Main Street, but she didn't care. She just wanted to get as far away as possible from Lyric. And from that... that *thing* that used to be her father.

Elizabeth was speeding along the highway when her phone buzzed. It was Tyler.

"What the heck is going on down there? First Jeremy, now you? Do I have to do everything myself?"

The image of Jeremy's blood on the floor and her father's black teeth played in a continuous loop in her mind. *It's in the water, Lizzie. I get so thirsty.*

Elizabeth took a long, deep breath and stammered, "The deal's gone s-south, sir. The families won't sign the lease. You need to get out here as soon as possible. Meet us at my father's house."

She hung up before Tyler could interrupt. She figured it was just as well that she didn't mention her father's policy against trespassers. After all, she wasn't on the Lyric account, and it would be a conflict of interest to say anything.

She kept on driving.

Released

by Caroline Grace
2013 Short Story 3rd Place Winner

The storm door banged with an exclamation mark as Sophie burst onto the front porch. "How can you hear yourself think out here, Grandma? That traffic is horrendous!"

"It keeps me from being lonely when you're not here. Reminds me there are people out there, comin' and goin'. Keeps me company, I guess."

"Well, I'm here today! Happy birthday, Grandma!" Sophie kissed her on the cheek.

"Thank you, dear. Sixty-nine doesn't feel so much different than sixty-eight, but I guess they all add up." Rebekah never missed a beat in the rhythm of the porch swing.

Sophie joined her on the swing. "Are you about ready to go? It's a long trip."

"Almost," Rebekah said.

"Do you have your list and map? Wouldn't you rather go somewhere fun? Every year, we take the same trip, and frankly, it's not a lot of fun. Let me take you out to eat, or maybe we could have a picnic."

Rebekah was slow to respond, "I have my list and map. I thought about going somewhere else, but I don't think I should. I owe it to Roseanne. Anyway, I thought we'd wait until after the mail comes. My new book might come today, and it will give me something to read."

"Grandma, it's a kid's book! What's it called… *Albert and the Map*? It'll take you like two seconds to read it. And for the record, you don't owe Roseanne anything. You're the only one who thinks you owe her something. You didn't even know her, and you visit her grave more than you do Grandpa's. It's over, Grandma -- it's been over for ten years. Let it go, okay?"

"You're talking too loud, dear. And *Albert, the List and the Map* is the one I already have. I ordered the second one. Anyway, we'll leave in a little while. I'm just not quite ready. It's my birthday, so give me a minute." Rebekah hesitated a moment, then continued, "And don't put Albert the Alligator down. You know my old stuffed Albert is sitting right there in the living room on the rocker, listening."

Rebekah's slight smile left Sophie wondering if she was joking.

Albert the Alligator had been Rebekah's favorite storybook character for as long as she could remember. As a little girl, she cuddled up to a stuffed Albert every night. As a student teacher, she dragged the much-loved Albert book into her classroom and read a little to her students each day. As a young married woman, the literary version of Albert had brought hours of mother-daughter bonding during story time.

Rebekah spoke again. "You could do with a little more *Albert the Alligator*, you know. He had a system and it worked for him. That was my favorite book growing up, and I actually took a lot of life principles from it. Do you remember what it was about?"

Sophie rolled her eyes. "Of course, I remember. You must have read it to me a hundred times."

Rebekah continued as though she hadn't heard. "The baby alligator, Albert, got lost and tried to find his way back to his family. Every time he received a new direction from someone along the way, he wrote it in his notebook, added it to his map, and headed off. Then he would say, 'I have a list and a map. What could possibly go wrong?' In the end, it served him well, and he found his family."

"Grandma, seriously, it's a kid's book. I'm not adopting principles from a book written for eight-year-olds, and I'm not sure you should, either." As soon as the words escaped her lips, Sophie wished she could inhale them, but the barrel had been opened, the conversation started, and it was too late. She had been down this road dozens of times before, and it never had a happy ending.

"You know Roseanne died because I didn't follow my list and map. I went to the grocery store first that day, and I was supposed to go there second, and Roseanne died because of it."

"It wouldn't have mattered when you went to the grocery," Sophie said with good intentions. "Grandma, please let's not go into this again."

Rebekah continued resolutely. "It happened

on my birthday, and it was Roseanne's birthday, too. It was ten years ago today, and we were exactly ten years apart in age. What are the odds of that? It's so spooky it's scary," she said, running her hands through her hair.

Sophie decided the only way out of the inevitable downward spiral was to let the conversation fade. She stood up and headed inside. "Would you like some lemonade, Grandma? I'm going to make some," she called back over her shoulder.

"No, thank you, I'm just going to rest a few minutes."

"Okay, I'll be back," she said, letting the door slam behind her as she went.

The porch swing swayed slowly back and forth. Early sunshine streaked across it and splattered shadows against the porch wall. Rebekah's slight frame snuggled into the maple swing, one foot underneath her, the other toe brushing the wooden floor just enough to hold the rhythm. Dressed in a honey-brown sweater and slacks with soft amber hair pulled up in a loose bun, the overall effect was a real-life study in monochrome. Rebekah closed brown eyes and leaned her head against the supporting swing chain.

The traffic on the corner was typically busy and loud, but it had been particularly erratic that morning. Nonetheless, the familiar sounds brought comfort to her. Eyes still closed, she listened to each sound in isolation as though they were instruments in an orchestra… a car without a muffler, a radio belting out an unfamiliar song through an open window, the roar of tires approaching, then passing by, a semi gearing up as the stoplight turned green. The traffic noises merged again into a single lullaby, and Rebekah let her mind drift.

As if by some premonition, her eyes flew open as she awakened from a state of half-sleep. She looked around for the cause of the interruption, at first thinking Sophie must have called her. She listened, but heard nothing. Still brooding, she looked out toward the traffic, then visually scanned the perimeter of her front yard. Seeing nothing amiss, she tried to shake off the unsettled feeling that enveloped her.

Just then, brakes screeched. Horns honked. Rebekah looked up just in time to see a red Ford Taurus speed through the stoplight, catching the tail of a little blue car, and spinning it around until it came to a halt, only to be rammed again from the other side by a black pickup truck.

Rebekah was out of her seat in a flash, spindly legs working independent of her brain, carrying her to the scene of the accident. She tugged on the little blue car's door handle to no avail.

"Roseanne! Roseanne!" she cried, peering inside the vehicle. "No, no, no… this can't be happening again …"

Sophie's voice carried over the din. "Grandma, get back! It's not Roseanne."

Time stood still as her mind tried to make sense of twisted metal, sirens, Sophie's faraway voice, honking horns, the distant sound of sobbing. Were they her sobs? Roseanne's? Sudden silence. Slow motion. Desperate hands silently yanked the car door to no avail. Voiceless people with moving mouths approached. Hurried cars screeched to a sudden halt without sound.

Sophie's voice breaking the silence. "Grandma, it's not Roseanne. It's someone else. The police are here, and you need to get back so they can help."

Then she felt Sophie's hands firmly gripping her arms, pulling her away from the blue car and back toward the house.

"I couldn't get her out, Sophie… let me get her out …"

Just as they reached the living room, Rebekah's knees buckled and darkness closed in. Her heart pounded in her ears as strong hands supported her.

"Grandma! Grandma! Come on, look at me… you're okay."

Rebekah felt tissues against her cheek, gently drying salty rivers of tears that emptied onto her neck. Somehow she was lying down now, away from the confusion. She heard her own voice, loud and plaintive. "Did they get out? Are they okay? Are they okay? Tell me!"

"It's okay ..."

"No, it's not okay! Tell me!" Why was her voice so hoarse?

"Grandma, I don't know, but I think they're okay. Shhh… be still."

Gentle hands pushed long strands of hair away from her eyes. It was Sophie… sweet Sophie, covering her up so her teeth wouldn't chatter. But she couldn't see.

"Eyes open. Come on, Rebekah. Open your eyes," said some logical voice in her head, but she was too tired to listen. With eyes still closed, Rebekah mustered the energy to speak. "She died. It was her birthday, and my birthday, and I ran a stoplight and hit her car and she died, Sophie… that lady, Roseanne, died on our birthdays. I lived, but she died."

"Grandma, that was a long time ago. We don't know the people in this wreck. You didn't hit them, and I don't think anyone died. It was just a car crash on the corner. Shhh… it's okay."

"Where's my list and map, Sophie?"

"Right here. I'm putting them in your hand."

"I went to the grocery store first and I was supposed to go there second, and Roseanne died because of it."

"The lights weren't working, Grandma. They were green in both directions. It wasn't your fault… just get some rest, okay?" Sophie helped her into bed, and the weight and warmth of her granddaughter's presence brought calm.

Restful sleep and productive dreams came to Rebekah, relieving the stress, calming the panic, soothing the body, organizing the mind. When she awoke, it was with a clarity and purpose she had not often possessed the last ten years.

"Sophie?"

Sophie appeared with a glass of water. "How do you feel? You've had a nice long nap. I hope it helped."

"Thanks, honey. I do feel better. There was a car crash on the corner, and I didn't have a very good reaction. Is that right?"

Sophie nodded as Rebekah continued. "I'm sorry. I know today's accident wasn't my fault. It's just that it happened on my birthday, so I was already thinking of Roseanne, and... I couldn't help myself. But, I *have* been thinking."

Sophie raised her eyebrows but said nothing.

"I don't feel much like going to Roseanne's grave today. It's been a hard day. It's a long way out in the country, and it's getting late. Besides, it truly was an accident. Do you think I should go see her today?"

"You don't need to go, Grandma. She'll understand."

"But Roseanne didn't have anyone, except two nieces. It may be that no one visits her except me."

"She won't miss you, Grandma. She's gone. You're going more for yourself than for her. It was your way of keeping the wound open, and punishing yourself, but it's over. You can let it go now. Oh, and guess what! Your book came in today's mail. Hang on, I'll get it."

Sophie placed the brown package in Rebekah's hands, and watched her open it.

"Look! A new publisher bought the rights to the Albert book and they're making it a series! This is the new one -- *Albert and the Absolutely Mad*

Adventure. Listen to this -- *Albert ditches his list and his map and goes on an unplanned adventure with his friend, Spiffy the Spider Monkey.*"

"Now that sounds like a life principle I could go with!" Sophie said with a smile.

"I think I'd like to take a trip tomorrow… to somewhere fun. You pick, and you can take me. I promise to leave my list at home, but maybe we should take the map, just in case. But I promise I won't open it."

Sophie squeezed her grandma tight. "Let's be sure and take Albert, too!"

The Marriage Proposal

by L. Edward Carroll
Short Story Contest Judge and CWI Tutor

At the sound of running feet, Tiffany didn't need to look up. It was Stanley Newton, the next-door neighbor, arms loaded with books, running to catch up. She quickened her pace.

Tall and gangly, he ran like a deranged ostrich. "Dang!" he gasped, as he caught up to her.

She sped up even more. As he started his usual jabbering, one of his notebooks slipped out and hit the sidewalk, spewing papers everywhere. As he stopped to pick them up, the rest of his books tumbled. On his knees, he scrambled to pick them up.

Spotting her fellow cheerleaders across the street, Tiffany saw her chance and made a dash, causing a car to come to a skidding halt, tires screaming. The driver laid on the horn. She lifted her shoulders, mimed the words, "I'm sorry," and ran across the street.

Startled by the sudden racket, Stanley looked up. When his beloved Tiffany skipped over the curb to greet her friends, he saw the driver make a lewd gesture. He ran at the car and beat his fists on the driver's window.

"Hey! What do you think you're doing? You almost ran over my girlfriend. You're crazy, you know that? They oughta revoke your license, you idiot!"

When the driver saw the tall, pimply-faced maniac with enough iron in his braces to build a small economy car screaming at him, he sped off, leaving Stanley in the middle of the road cursing and waving impotent fists. He glanced up, expecting Tiffany's grateful reaction, but she and her cheerleader friends were already down the block, laughing and pointing at him as they disappeared into the school's front entrance. Stanley's pale face looked even whiter contrasted with the mass of angry red acne pustules.

"Does that jerk follow you everywhere?" one of her friends asked.

"It's like living in the movie, Ground Hog Day. Day after day, that Ichabod Crane look-alike catches up with me. His big Adam's apple bobs while he chatters incessantly, like I care what he's saying! I've tried every dodge I can think of. Walking to school earlier and earlier didn't work, neither did jogging. I think he waits for me to pass his house. On the walk home after school, I hear his running footsteps and cringe. When I have after-school activities, he waits. He really creeps me out, know what I mean?

Her girlfriends rollicked with laughter.

"And get this… my mother says, 'Honestly, I don't see why you complain so much about his walking with you. He's such a nice, polite boy. He wouldn't hurt a fly.' Dad says I should get to know him, and that he's going to Yale a year after me.

'You worry too much,' he says. How great is that? Now I dread going to Yale."

"You do great impersonations, Tiff. Did anyone ever tell you that?" And all the girls laughed.

The next day, an old blue Ford pickup sat in Tiffany's driveway. Curious, she looked out the big front bay window. Her father burst through the front door. "Hey, Punkin, catch," he shouted.

Speechless, she looked at the ring of keys in her hand.

"Oh, Dad, it's mine?" She gave him a big hug and kissed his cheek. "You're the best!"

"But before you drive, kiddo, we're going to talk."

When she ran out to survey her property, her mother wasn't so cheerful. "Oh, I don't know about this, Maurice. Are you sure?"

"Yes. I'm sure."

The next day, Stanley was clever and proved he could adapt his routine with ease. As sure as rain, there he was the next morning, waiting for her in the school parking lot.

Tiffany parked the truck and decided to tell him what she really thought.

"Look, you're a nice guy and all that, but I'm not interested in you as a boyfriend. I never have been, nor will I ever be, so please…"

But everything after the word "please" became a buzzing in his ears. He entered a dark place and folded himself up inside. Stanley hunched his shoulders forward, slowly turned, and fast-walked home, his head so far forward it looked as if he would fall on his face.

"Stanley, what's wrong?" his mother said.

"Nothing, Mom. Just tired."

"I'll make you some hot chocolate and cookies, dear. Go rest. I'll bring them up." She was used to his curious "trances," as she called them, and the next day, she phoned the school and made excuses for his absence.

That evening, Tiffany's mother called his mother. "I think your daughter has an overactive imagination," Stanley's mother said. "When I was a young debutante, I used to think the same thing about some of the boys, but I'll talk to him." But that promise was never kept.

After a Stanley-free week, Tiffany began to relax and enjoy her liberty. Why, she wondered, had she had ever waited so long to be direct with him? Her self-confidence climbed a few notches. Now she was free to think about summer vacation and shopping for her new wardrobe for Yale. She read brochures about campus life and thoughts of starting a new life with new friends lifted her spirits.

Stanley, however, couldn't get Tiffany out of his mind. While he languished in his room for a week, he dreamed of her softly flowing reddish-blonde hair bouncing on her shoulders as she walked. Her shocking emerald green eyes haunted his steps and penetrated his heart, making it sing on the rare times when she actually looked at him.

She has the smoothest, lightly tanned skin I've ever seen on any girl. Those full lips are just waiting to kiss me, he thought. Why doesn't she offer me a ride in her truck? Her dad probably gave her a lecture on responsibility and insurance. She doesn't give rides to anyone. He won't let her. That dratted, poopy truck. I miss walking with her.

"I have to find a way to be near her," he muttered to himself. "Time is the real enemy. It'll be a whole year before I can join her at Yale. Once she gets in college and meets some smooth-talking senior, my chances will be gone. She loves that truck. If I put sugar in the tank… no. She'd guess it was me. She'd never speak to me again. If that happened, I'd kill myself."

He stopped and looked into a wall mirror. He felt a little silly talking to himself all the time. Long into the night, Stanley worked to solve his problem before graduation. He was a straight-A-student and was in the habit of making lists. Everything had to be perfect.

"Tomorrow's Friday," he said to himself. "She's a volunteer for slow learning students, so she'll be the last one out of the parking lot."

He lurked in the shadows and watched her every move. On Friday, June 3, just three school days before graduation, he put his plan into action. He muttered, "I have a list and a map. What can possibly go wrong?"

In the school parking lot, the truck's overhead cab light burned dimly as Tiffany filed her students' papers into her briefcase. She caught a movement out of the corner of her eye when a figure appeared out of the evening gloom. Her heart raced and she started her truck, ready to leave in a hurry. When

Stanley came into the light, he held a dozen red roses wrapped in a cellophane cone in one hand, and held the other hand behind his back. He galumphed purposely toward her truck, grinning. She rolled the window down and gave a wary smile.

"Stanley! You nearly scared me to death." Maybe he came to apologize. He must have a card or a box of candy behind his back. How sweet, but how do I say 'thank you' without encouraging him?

He looked into the open window and glanced at her cheerleader's short, short white pleated skirt that revealed too much of her smooth thighs, and immediately looked away.

She must have come straight from cheerleading practice to her tutoring class and didn't have time to change into decent clothes. He was disgusted with himself for what he was thinking. He shoved the flowers at her and blurted out, "Tiffany, will you marry me?"

Tiffany covered her mouth with both hands and emitted a nervous giggle until the giggles turned into uncontrolled laughter.

The blood drained from his face and his acne flared into fiery red splotches. He flung the red roses to the pavement where they scattered in all directions. He brought his hidden arm around from behind his back. Tiffany's face changed to horror as he reached into the open window with his father's nickel-plated Smith and Wesson .38 snub-nose revolver and mashed the trigger until he spent all five bullets.

He was careful though. He made sure not to

shoot her beautiful face. The lifeblood quickly blossomed like a red rose and soaked through the front of her white school sweater with a blue letter "N" on the front, for Northrop High. As her life gushed out, she slumped over the steering wheel, quite dead. Her red-blonde hair flowed prettily around the steering wheel.

His ears were ringing. Surely his eardrums had burst. He had brought the gun to use on himself if she rejected him, but she had done the worst thing possible. She had laughed. Agitated, he raced around the truck, opened the passenger door and dragged her to the passenger side of the bench seat. Placing her in a natural sitting position, he strapped her body in and swooped her hair back. Searching through her briefcase, he found what he needed and with several quick wraps, scotch-taped her head to the headrest before he slammed the door. Backing out of the parking lot, the sharp smell of gun smoke mingled with the pungent odor of burning rubber and lingered in the air several minutes.

Little Charles Moran, one of Tiffany's "slow" students, was also struck with a severe case of adolescent puppy love. He watched the target of his torment as she entered her truck, and was about to leave when Stanley pulled out the gun and shot her. Charlie went into shock for a few minutes before gathering his thoughts, and ran back to the school where he pounded on locked doors and yelled for help. Next, he ran to the nearest house, where he called the police.

Meanwhile, just outside of town, Stanley

slowed and cruised by the teen hangout where the popular kids from Northrop High gathered on Friday nights. Graceful young women on roller skates took orders and expertly delivered food to the trays attached to the driver's side window. Stanley made a leisurely circuit around the parked cars, enjoying the air that was deliberately infused with the aroma of burgers and fries by large fans.

As the Everly Brothers' Wake up Little Suzie blared over the speakers, Stanley snapped his fingers and bobbed his head a little out of sync to the beat. Some of Tiffany's friends waved at the familiar shiny Blue Ford, F150 pickup truck. Freshly washed and waxed, it sparkled under the bright lights. When Tiffany's friends honked in recognition, Stanley rolled down his window and broke into an enormous metallic smile, laughing insanely at the surprised looks when they realized who was driving. He waved back, then pulled onto the main street and sped out of town with Tiffany at his side.

"I'm going to join you, Tiffany, just as soon as I reload the gun. You just sit back and enjoy the ride."

In a state of bliss, Stanley was unaware of the wailing of many sirens and the long string of flashing red and blue lights bearing down on the blue Ford truck.

*This story is derived from a true incident. The characters' names are fictitious, as is the name of the high school.

Looking for Gracie

by Lin Treadgold
Award Winning Guest Author

My phone is probably the most useful thing I own. I can Skype, I use Facebook, and if I am feeling vain, I use the camera to take "selfies," but a mobile phone can also bring news of the worst kind.

"Put your hand on your heart and tell me it isn't true. Martin, please, is she…?"

I listened to his voice explaining how he'd put her to bed and kissed her goodnight.

"Okay, she's not in her bed. Should I come over?"

I listened again to his torment and made a thin attempt to calm him.

"Relax, I'm sure she will be fine, she won't be far away. I'll meet you in half an hour."

I slid the phone into my pocket and grabbed a sandwich. I knew it was going to be a long night. I dressed in my jeans and t-shirt and left the house as quickly as possible.

Gracie, you silly child. Where are you for God's sake? As she was my niece, I had a duty to help find her. I put the keys in the ignition and set out to Portland Bay.

At two in the morning, I hadn't even put my finger on the doorbell when Martin opened the door and almost fell into my arms.

"Clara, I'm frantic. We have to do something. The police will be here soon."

"The police? Where did you last see her?"

"She was in bed. You know how she sleepwalks. I got up to visit the bathroom and looked in her room – she was gone! I've searched the house, the garden, and she's nowhere to be found. You can't talk to her when she's in that state. You have to find her, and guide her back to bed. I'm always scared I may frighten her."

"Okay, let's think about where she usually goes. We have to think like a five-year old. How about the park? The swings? The roundabout? Write down all the places where I could help you look and… why the heck don't you lock your doors at night, Martin?"

"I thought I had, but obviously I hadn't. Oh, Clara, where could she be?"

"Okay, let's start with the park. Then where?"

"I worry she might have gone down to the beach, but it's a bit far for a kid that age. I guess she wouldn't remember how to get there."

"I'm not ruling it out. Where else?"

"You could try calling Nancy. Her daughter, Jessica, plays with Gracie."

"Give me the number."

I carried on, adding to the list, until I had ten possible places we could look. The doorbell rang.

"Mr. Thirkell. Martin Thirkell?"

"Oh, thank goodness you came. Come in. This is my sister, Clara."

I acknowledged the presence of the two police officers in uniform.

"Gracie is a sleepwalker. I'm having a difficult time right now. My wife, Joanne, she… she passed away last year. She had…." He shook his head. "I know Gracie misses her."

I listened to the break in his voice.

"Where have you looked, Mr Thirkell?"

"Everywhere. Absolutely everywhere I can think of. I also looked in both sheds in the garden. The front door was open. You don't think… God, I hope no one has taken her."

The doorbell rang again. It was Nancy.

"Is there anything I can do?" she said.

"You can help me if you want. If two of us are looking, we stand a better chance of finding her."

"Stay as calm as you can, Mr. Thirkell. We'll search the streets as well," the police sergeant said. "We'll keep you informed."

"You stay here, Martin, in case she comes home. I hear people can do all kinds of things when they sleepwalk; drive cars, make a meal, and it's quite possible she will find her own way back," I said.

"Clara, she's only five years old. She won't be able to navigate home again, let alone drive a car or cook a gourmet meal! Do you know this area since we moved up here? It's not like Dorset."

"Of course I do. I don't live that far away." Impatience and panic had always been one of his less appealing traits.

"Okay, okay, sorry."

"Please try to stay calm. I have a list and a map. What could possibly go wrong?"

"*Everything's* gone wrong, Clara! Please just get out there and see if you can find her."

"Okay. Stay calm."

"That's easy for you to say."

"I brought a flask of coffee in case we get chilled," Nancy said. "Where should we start?"

"The park. We'll try there first."

"Here, take these," Martin said. You'll need flashlights. I bought new batteries the other day."

"Call me if there are any changes. My mobile is charged," I said.

"Just go, Clara, the longer you wait, the worse it could be."

Before I left the house, the phone rang and Martin answered it. I waited to see if it was the police.

"Hi, Paula. Yes, I thought you might. It's Gracie. She's missing, on one of her sleepwalks."

I gazed quizzically at Martin. He put his hand over the receiver for a moment. "It's Paula from next door. She wants to know why the police are here."

He carried on talking to Paula. I left the house. Perhaps Paula could support Martin while we were out.

Nancy got out of the car first. We scanned the park benches with our flashlights and a fox jumped off the wall of the school playground beyond. We called Gracie's name many times and listened, but nothing came in reply. The swings swayed in a light sea breeze and we both decided no one could possibly be there.

"Okay, where next?" Nancy asked.

"Let's try the schoolyard. She used to go to the nursery, and her mother always walked her there, three days a week."

"Yes, I remember." Nancy smiled.

The empty schoolyard was now devoid of happy children who were all, except Gracie, tucked in bed. After an hour, we returned to the car and perused the map.

"Let's try the beach," I said. We drove down the promenade and shone the lights from the car to the shoreline. Nothing, except…

"Oh, my gosh. See that?" I dipped the headlights for modesty.

"I'm not looking." Nancy giggled. "They're obviously up to no good."

"Well, they seem to be enjoying it," I tittered as I turned the car around.

We search three hours and the thought of not finding Gracie filled our minds with painful despondency. We had now visited all the places on our list, scoured the local streets, and checked all the places a child may like to play. Nothing, except the occasional car, moving slowly up the street. A couple of women wearing short skirts and high heels stood outside the cinema. It was then that a lump came to my throat. What if someone had picked her up, and… no, I couldn't think about that. I phoned Martin, but he confirmed there was no further news.

"Come on, let's go back. No news is sometimes good news," Nancy said.

We drove back and met a man with a rucksack on his back. I stopped and asked if he'd seen a small child. Nancy reminded me that if he had, he would have contacted the police. I was desperate to give Martin some good news.

Five police cars parked on the corner of Martin's road. By then it was daybreak and five in the morning.

"Any news?" I said, but by the look on Martin's face, I knew nothing had happened. My heart sank. Gracie would be very cold by now. It was summer but the evenings were chilly.

"Nothing," Martin said. His eyelids drooped as he spoke. "Paula's been here most of the night. We phoned everyone we know. She's been very good to me since Joanne…"

"Have you eaten?" I asked.

"No. How can I eat with all this going on?"

"I'll make some breakfast."

Nancy piped up. "Sorry, Clara, I have to get back for Bert. He has to go to work, and I must get Jessica to school. I'll come back later." Nancy sighed at her own fatigue and left us.

"Thanks, Nancy. I couldn't have done it without you," I called down the street and went inside to find Martin on the phone again.

"Yes, we've looked in there, too," I heard him say, and he pressed the button on his iPhone.

"We have to let the police do their job now," I said.

I gazed at Martin. Sisters and brothers don't usually hug in our family, but I reckoned now was the time to do it. I put my arms around him. "I know she's going to be all right, Martin. I know it." I heard a cough. "Did you hear that?"

"What?"

"A noise—like someone coughing. Hush, listen!"

"It's nothing."

I listened again, but he was right. It was just my imagination running wild, as usual. "Let's go upstairs, look in her room, and see if we can find any clues," I said.

I followed Martin up to the landing and into Gracie's small pink bedroom with teddy bears and dolls lined across the dressing table. The scrunched-up covers revealed it was just a bed without a person inside it. He glanced at the empty space for a moment. I looked underneath, but no Gracie.

"I don't see anything, do you? She wasn't even wearing her dressing gown. Poor kid will be frozen. I can't bear to think about it," he said.

"Come on. Let's go downstairs and have some coffee."

As we passed by the hall, Martin stopped. "Just remembered. I have a more recent photo I can give the police."

He searched his jacket on the peg in the hall. "Where's my wallet? I always keep it in my jacket pocket." He pushed the lounge door wide where he'd been watching a David Attenborough film earlier that evening. "Let's see if they have it on the news yet," he said as he entered the lounge. "Where's the TV? It's gone! We've been burgled, and I think they stole my wallet. Oh no, no, it can't be! I think they took Gracie with them."

Martin's face turned pale with shock and he dashed outside to tell the police, who were already setting up an incident room.

I sat at the kitchen table with my head in my hands. Again, I heard a cough, and this time I knew I hadn't imagined it. "Gracie, are you there? Is that you? It's Auntie Clara."

I searched all the rooms, but there was no sign of her. In the spare room, I was desperate to lie down on the bed, but told myself I must stay awake. Did I hear movement? I looked around. Someone was watching me. The hairs on the back of my neck stood to attention. What if the burglar was still there? "Gracie, is that you?"

I heard a faint sniff coming from below. I looked under the bed, and there she was, all curled up and looking very frightened.

"Oh, Gracie, why are you under the bed?" I pulled her out of the cramped space. "It's no wonder Daddy couldn't find you."

"I found her!" I shouted. "I found her!"

It was a low bed with drawers, and a gap in between. No one dreamed she could fit in the space underneath.

"Hi, Auntie Clara. I was asleep when the man came. I was standing on the top of the stairs when I woke up. I didn't like him, and I told him not to take Daddy's fings away or I would scream really,

really loud like Mummy said. He ran out the door very fast."

"What man?"

"The man that came in our house. I ran upstairs and hid under the bed. I was a likkel bit frightened. He wasn't very nice. I found Oscar asleep under the bed and we snuggled togevver to keep warm."

"Have you been under the bed all night with the kitty?"

Her cheeks almost matched the pink of her pajamas.

"Yes. I fink so. Sometimes I hide in here for fun, but I go downstairs at night. Daddy said sometimes I fall asleep standing up. I love you lots, Auntie Clara."

I realized that if she had screamed, Martin would have been there immediately. Gracie's screams were loud enough to wake the whole neighborhood. Instead, she had put her own life in danger, or maybe was too scared to scream, but her threats were enough to chase the thief away. My heart filled with pride and sheer relief.

"I love you, too, Gracie." I held her close and tears ran down my cheeks. She snuggled into my neck and sucked her thumb while I smoothed blonde curls away from tired eyes. "It's going to be all right. You were a very brave girl! I bet Mummy would have been very proud of you."

BIO: Lin Treadgold is a romance author who

lives in the Netherlands, but plans to retire to Devon in the south west of the UK in 2015. She is a member of the Society of Authors and the Romantic Novelists' Association. She began her writing career when her husband was offered a job in Holland. After owning a driver training business for 25 years, starting over with a new vocation in a foreign country was daunting, but she saw it through.

Lin has travelled the world several times and has plenty of stories to entertain her readers. Her book, *Goodbye, Henrietta Street,* a contender for the Joan Hessayon Award in 2014, was published last year and she has two more books in progress.

Visit her website to learn more:
www.itslinhere.wordpress.com.

What If?

by Emily-Jane Hills Orford
Guest Author and CWI Tutor

"What if?" Margaret muttered to herself as she trudged through the snow, making her way home from work. "What if?" she grumbled as she slipped in the slush.

"What if?" She shook her head. Too many what ifs. Life was full of them. This particular *what if* sounded so promising. Could she really make her father believe her? After all, it would only cost $1.00 to find out. Could she afford $1.00? It might be worth the sacrifice, the risk.

Margaret thought, *I have a list and a map. What could possibly go wrong?* She had seen the list of lots that were up for sale. She had seen the map, the layout of plans. What could possibly go wrong? She could feel it in her bones. It was a good risk to take, one that would provide her with unknown benefits for many years to come. However, there was always that *what if*. If something could go wrong, it probably would.

"Father," she started rehearsing to herself, "a gentleman came into the office today. He was selling lots of land in Calgary. It's only $1.00 an acre." Mr. Lockheed had been very enthusiastic and very persuasive. Margaret thought back to his presentation to the office staff. All of the girls had listened intently and many had quickly offered the fee from their pay cheque. It was hard-earned money, and $1.00 was a big chunk out of the weekly pay. How convenient that Mr. Lockheed had arrived at Goldie's on payday.

Margaret knew better. She knew her pay went directly to her father and she was provided with a small allowance to buy much needed essentials, like new stockings. She always needed new stockings, it seemed.

Maps. She had always been so sure of herself, mapping out her life, making lists of what she wanted to do, where she wanted to be in ten years' time, twenty years, and so on. Life was all about making lists to see that things were accomplished, and making plans, like a map. Or *not* making lists and plans. That was the other part of the equation, the *not*, the *what could possibly go wrong* – the unknown variable that made so many twists and turns, inevitably heaving havoc on the best of lists, the best of maps, and the best of plans.

Her father was one of those variables. Just thinking about him and his often too down-to-earth realism made her want to give up right then and there. She was beginning to doubt her resolve. If she could convince him it was a good investment, and it was a very big *if*, that dollar would probably have to come from her allowance and not the big chunk that father kept as her contribution to the running of the family home.

"Hmm!" Margaret huffed. Perhaps it was a scam after all. Should she even bother to broach the subject with her father?

"Women should never be allowed to handle money," he was forever saying, defending his actions with archaic notions of a woman's place in society. "Women are good for only one thing, taking care of the family and the home."

She didn't agree, but what could she do? Her income was insufficient to support herself. Living at home was convenient and inexpensive. Unfortunately, living at home also resulted in heated arguments.

"It's 1920, Father," she had said with a storm. "Women can do much more than just run a home, have babies and raise a family. They can be doctors and lawyers. They can be whatever they want to be."

"Such a waste!" Father always forced his opinions on anyone who would listen. Maybe he thought he could turn back the clock and remake the world as he thought it should be. "Why would anyone in their right mind want to invest in an education for a girl?" he said. Everything should be in its proper place, Father advocated, just like a map. But on his map, a woman stayed at home.

Margaret had wanted to go to nursing school in Toronto. She was good at taking care of people and the local doctor said she would make a good nurse, but Father would have none of it. Even though she had stellar marks, she wasn't even allowed to take an academic program in high school. Instead, she took a two-year secretarial course that prepared her for the job she now held at

Goldie's. She had worked hard. She always did. At eighteen, she was already the boss' personal secretary, and not too popular with other women in the office who had vied for the much coveted position.

She made a good salary, even if she saw so little of it. She stamped her feet as she felt, once again, the unfairness of the situation. If only she had been born a boy! Then she could have done whatever she wanted in life. Then the *what ifs* would have been surmountable, and the *what could possibly go wrong* would not even be in the equation.

As a boy, she could have done no wrong in her father's eyes, like her younger brother, Jim, but Margaret knew otherwise. He was a scoundrel, a lazy boy who always looked for the easy way out, yet he would receive the higher education if he would buckle down and do more studying and less drinking. That was Jim's biggest vice. His other vice, which would probably be his downfall, was women.

Reaching the bottom of the steep hill, Margaret stopped to take a breath. It was an effort to climb at the best of times. Looking behind her, she saw the Grand River rushing along, coursing its path through the Galt Valley. The valley was very much what it suggested, with steep hills on either side of the river. Ten years ago, when her family had moved here from Scotland, the community had been much smaller, situated more in the valley, closer to the banks of the river. Galt had grown and, with its growth, more houses had been built. Many of these now nestled into the steep incline of the hills. The list of people that populated the community had also grown, as had the map. What could possibly go wrong? For the community, it seemed nothing at all. It just kept growing and prospering. If only her life could be so simple, so straightforward, like this road that led straight uphill toward home.

With another sigh, Margaret started up its slippery slope. The hill was her metaphor for all of the obstacles that she confronted on a daily basis, particularly her father. He was her biggest hill, forever restricting her movement and her life. He was always the *what could possibly go wrong?*

Should she even bother to broach the subject of the lands in Calgary? Nothing ventured, nothing gained, her mother always said. Could she make an impression on her father? Or would she just be giving him more reason to defend his belief that women should never be allowed to handle money?

I have a list. Well, sort of. *I have a map,* she reminded herself as she placed one foot in front of the other with great determination. Or, at least she saw the map. If this investment proved worthy of Mr. Lockheed's promotion, then her list could very well come to fruition. *What could possibly go wrong?* Everything? Nothing? Only time would tell. Or, more accurately, only Father would tell.

Margaret reached the top of the hill and turned along her street toward home. She was warm. It was quite a hike from the office. Inward stress mounted from internal strife. Almost at her destination, she still couldn't make up her mind. As she reached the walk to her front door, she braced herself, straightened her shoulders, and marched up the steps and inside.

"Is that you, Margaret?" her father called from the sitting room.

"Yes, Father," Margaret called back as she took off her winter coat, then bent over to untie wet boots.

"Come in here, please," her father called.

"Yes, Father," Margaret replied. "Just as soon as I have taken care of my wet things."

She took her time tidying her mess. The boots had brought in a trail of slush and Margaret knew that she had to wipe it up quickly before her mother snapped at her. Mother's house was meticulously clean, and people had to clean up their own mess. Finally, she took a deep breath, braced herself and walked smartly into the sitting room.

"You took long enough," Father said in a grumble. Before she could reply, he carefully folded his newspaper and placed it on the table beside his chair. Everything in this house was done with precision and care, even something as mundane as folding a newspaper. "I hear there was a visitor to the offices this morning."

Margaret groaned inwardly. *Did nothing escape him?* Now her decision was made for her. She would have to discuss the land issue.

"I hope you had sense not to believe all that rubbish," he snapped. "I understand this Mr. Lockheed managed to manipulate money from several feeble-minded office girls. Foolishness, if you ask me. They will never see their money again, and Mr. Lockheed is all the richer for it."

"It is an investment, Father," Margaret said. "Mr. Lockheed says Calgary will be a booming center in no time, and the money we invest will more than double."

"Rubbish!" Father snorted. "I cannot believe that you even listened to him, let alone believed him. Do you even know where Calgary is?"

"Yes, Father."

Before Margaret could say more, he continued. "It's way out west. Cattle country, I hear. Ranches and country people. Dry, arid land. Nothing else there. No big city is going to grow out there. What utter nonsense! Don't be fooled by what that man says. Your money is better kept in a bank than investing in land far across the country."

"Times are changing, Father," Margaret interjected. "Large cities are appearing all over this country. I could make a list of all the booming communities across the country and show you a recent map that depicts even more cities than appeared on last year's map."

"Perhaps," he said, not enjoying the knowledge that his daughter was free to display. Women shouldn't be as smart as Margaret and, if they were, they shouldn't show it off in front of the man of the house.

"How do you know for sure that Calgary will become a large city?" he asked. Before Margaret could answer, he said, "Aha! You don't know, do you? Forget what you heard today, and don't even think of giving that man $1.00! Rest assured, I will know if you do." Shaking his head, he retrieved his paper. "Women!" he muttered, carefully unfolding the paper on his lap. "They have no sense at all when it comes to money!"

"And what if, twenty or thirty years down the road, it turns out that I could have made a lot of money on my purchased acre of land?" she asked.

"That will never happen, so forget about it. One cannot live on dreams and what ifs."

"Yes, Father," Margaret sighed. "But someday I'll prove you wrong. If not about this, then about something else."

"Be mindful who you're speaking to, young lady!" Father looked at her sternly over the top of his paper. "I'm still the man in this house and, as long as you live here, you will do as I say."

I have a list and a map. What could possibly go wrong? But aloud, she responded as expected. "Yes, Father." She turned and walked to the kitchen. "But I'll have my say in the end," she muttered to herself as soon as she was out of earshot. "Just you wait and see. Then you'll be wondering, like me, *what if.* What if the list of potentially profitable plots was really well worth the property on the map of Calgary? Other than the risk to my $1.00, what could possibly go wrong?"

A Fork in the Road

by Stuart Aken
Award Winning Guest Author

Lauren tapped the steering wheel in irritation, following the beat of unfamiliar music on the radio. Where was Jessica? She knew time was limited. This was too much. She'd have to leave the car and run through the cloudburst to get her daughter.

"Sorry, Mum. Couldn't find my keys." She got in, dripping rain as she tossed her light coat on the back seat.

"I was beginning to think you'd got lost." Lauren said. She started the engine and pulled away.

"Not going to drive at this speed, are you? We don't have much time."

Lauren peered through water streaming down the windscreen in spite of the double speed wipers. "I like to see the road ahead, dear. You know, so I don't kill some poor unsuspecting pedestrian."

Jessica shrugged. "You're driving."

"Indeed, I am. You know where you're headed?"

Jessica merely looked at her mother.

"And you have what you need?" Lauren said.

Jessica sighed. "I have a list and a map."

"What could possibly go wrong!" Lauren finished for her.

It lightened the mood and they both laughed.

For a while, they drove in silence, the unfamiliar tracks on the radio matching the unknown route.

"I didn't know you liked this station, Mum."

"I don't. It's for you."

"Oh. Right."

Again, that uncomfortable silence fell between them, music fighting the noise of rain as they plowed through the storm. Another fork in the road came and went without comment from Jessica and the road narrowed a little more. Lauren squinted through coursing water, searching for signs. The main road seemed to go straight on, so she continued on that track. Through the smear of rain, she thought the road continued straight, and passed a bend to the right. Almost at once, she discovered another bend ahead and had to slow to take it, wrenching the car around abruptly so they didn't leave the road. Jessica sighed.

"I'm sorry, dear. I know this isn't what you wanted. But your father and I felt it would be better this way. Look on it as a…"

"…challenge, Mother? You don't think I've had enough of those already?"

Lauren wanted to stop, put her arms around her only child, comfort her, but time was against them. If they didn't reach the city by lunchtime, they wouldn't make the connection, or at least would have no time to buy the essentials beforehand.

"I wanted to take you to lunch before we shop."

"That's nice. Italian?"

"I hope we'll have the time, now."

Jessica thumped the dash in front of her. "Mother. I told you. I was out last night with friends. Saying goodbye, you know? Mentioning the fact, I may never see them again. Of course, we were late getting back. I had to finish packing this morning."

The rain had slowed to a mere deluge and Lauren felt able to speed up a little. Perhaps they would make it in time after all. They'd passed several turns, both left and right, but Jessica had made no comment, although Lauren was fairly certain they should be passing the hills to their left rather than approaching them. It was all new country to her. Her journey to Jessica's shared accommodation had been from the other side of town and she'd never driven out this way before.

"You do understand why we want to make the move, don't you, dear?"

"Of course I do. I just wish you could've given me another six months. I could've found somewhere else to live before going off on my own."

"I thought you wanted an adventure. I mean, all that studying and hard work. You need a break from books and computer screens. You've been planning this, saving for it more than a year."

Jessica nodded. "That's when I thought I'd be travelling with Glenda or, better yet, with Jamie. Now, she's marrying that moron instead. And Jamie, well, you know about him. I didn't expect to have to do it by myself. I won't know a soul, and it's thousands of miles away."

"If you really don't want to go, why didn't you say so? We thought you were keen on it. You don't have to go. Come and live at home. Move with us."

"Don't slow down. I'll miss the flight, and I still have things to buy before I board."

"You're still determined to go, then?"

"Take no notice of my whining, Mum. I'm just nervous. I was expecting to travel with someone and now I'm flying off to the wilds by myself. I'm edgy, that's all. Take no notice. Where are we?"

Lauren shrugged. "No idea. You're navigating, dear."

"I thought you knew the way."

"I've never been here before. I told you that."

"You really don't know the way?"

"Check your map."

"Map?"

"You said you had a list and a…"

"…map. Yes. A list of things I need to buy and a map of Australia so I know where I'm going when I get there."

"Oh. So you've no idea where we are now?"

"Why would I? You said you'd drive me to the airport. Naturally, I assumed you knew where it was."

Lauren slowed down. Stopped the car.

"Why are you stopping? We don't have time, and…"

"There's no point driving when we may be going in the wrong direction. Get me the map book, Jessica. It's on the back seat."

The younger woman stretched over the back

of her seat and Lauren noticed just how much her daughter had grown. She turned to study her and realized she was a very attractive girl, a young woman to be proud of.

"I love you, you know."

"It's not here. What did you say, Mum?"

Lauren shook her head. "No matter. The book's not there? Maybe your father's got it, for the trip to the new house."

"Like that's going to happen. Now what?"

Lauren turned off the radio. "Can't think with that racket going on. Doesn't your mobile have some sort of map program?"

"App, you mean." Jessica dug in her bag and dredged her phone from its depths. She held it up, looked at the screen, and scanned the area. "No signal. We're miles from anywhere, Mum."

"We'll have to turn around and go back the way we came. See if we can find a signpost or maybe somewhere that modern technology will actually work!"

"I didn't change things, Mum. I can't help it if you don't like things the way they are. But my generation didn't make the changes."

Lauren, already too conscious of her own demographics' responsibility for much that was wrong with the world, let the comment pass.

"And what's the point of turning around now, Mum? We know the airport's in this general direction, don't we? Might as well keep going 'til we find a sign. The rain's easing; we might even be able to see it!"

Lauren set off again, with little confidence that this minor road would lead to the airport, which sat on the edge of a major city, but what else could she do? For the next few miles, they drove in a silence broken only by the occasional splash of a flood on the road and the hypnotic swish of windscreen wipers. The road wound into the hills and Lauren grew more certain they were heading in the wrong direction. This was an isolated part of the country and they should be on a major road if they were to find the airport. Still, with Jessica in her current mood, it was easier to go along with her wishes.

"Any signal yet, dear?"

"Out here? You must be joking. They still think the telly has little people in it, you know."

Lauren laughed at the hyperbole but then realized her daughter wasn't kidding. "You're not serious!"

Jessica studied her. "One of the girls I was sharing with comes from around here. Says her next door neighbor won't have a telly because he won't have those little people in his house."

"She was joking, dear."

"Nope. They're real backward."

"Really backward."

"Please, Mum. I'm not at school. I've got a degree. I don't need lessons in grammar."

Lauren nodded; it was one of her bad habits. A reflex that made her correct improper grammar. The result of more than thirty years spent teaching English.

"Look, there's a sign. Slow down and we'll see

what it says," Jessica said.

They pulled up and read names of villages on the fingerpost, its weathered pointers giving four possible directions. None of the names were familiar, and carried no clues as to what lay beyond.

"We're lost, aren't we?"

"It appears so. Shall we turn around?"

Jessica shrugged. "Whatever we do, I won't have time for lunch with you, not even to buy the sunscreen I want. If we're lucky, we'll get there in time to see my plane take off."

"It isn't like you to be so down, Jess. Is there something you haven't told me?"

"Don't be so stupid!" She wrenched the door open and stormed off into the rain.

Lauren sat a moment, stunned. What was that all about? Then she realized Jessica had left the car without her coat. She'd be soaked in seconds. She pulled onto the grass and felt the car sink a little as it left the harder road surface. Struggling into her own coat, she followed her daughter's progress along one of the turnings at this crossroads, almost dropping the other coat as she did so. Jess was already a few hundred yards away, walking with her head down, oblivious of the pouring rain. Lauren began to run, concerned to get her under some protection against the chill, wind and rain.

The open land about her, dotted with small patches of stunted and wind-blown trees, and sporting pools of open water on the few flat surfaces rose steeply toward a sky yet dark with more rain. The road, poorly surfaced and maintained, was drowned in places by wide puddles that stretched the whole width. She was forced to splash through them, soaking her shoes and feet.

"Jessica! Jessica, please wait."

But the exasperating child surged forward with no regard for mother or weather. Lauren paused, panting from unaccustomed exercise, and then set off again at a brisk walk. She glanced back. The curve in the road and slope of the hillside had already hidden the car. She shivered in the chilling wind.

An abrupt turn and dip made her daughter vanish and Lauren dashed forward to maintain contact. When she topped the small rise where Jessica had last been in sight, there was no sign of her.

"Jessica? Jess! Where are you?"

No reply. No sign of her daughter. She ran again, seeking the point where she'd last seen her. The wind strengthened and rain soaked unprotected hair, dripping down her face and obscuring vision further. She began to tremble, unspecified fear mingling with the cold and wet. Where had she gone?

Stumbling down into the dip, she looked about, searching for any sign of Jessica. It was impossible for the girl to have disappeared without a trace. A small brook ran on either side of the dip, passed under the road, and tumbled white water into a deep gully. Gingerly, anxiety moving her with slow purpose, she looked over the edge of the roadway into the point where the rushing stream passed under the road. No sign of Jessica. She crossed broken tarmac and stared down into the gully. Nothing. Just fast flowing water falling down a steep slope lined with small bushes and dwarf trees.

"Jess! Jessica? Where are you?"

Frightened now, unable to think straight, she looked back along her route. Of course, the girl wasn't behind her. That was stupid. But the car was back there. Should she go back, drive to this point, and start the search again? She stepped back a pace, unsure. Suppose Jess was hurt or had fallen? Or was she just out of sight?

Lauren moved forward again and spotted where the road climbed a short, steep rise. Judging by the hillside, it must take an equally steep drop and turn a corner.

Lauren paused and calmed herself with deep breaths. No need to panic. It was a wild landscape but nothing dangerous lurked here. Only the weather and the strangeness of an unknown land. Everything would be fine. She'd top that hill and catch sight of Jessica down the other side. The girl hadn't heard her call through the wind and rain. That was all.

She moved forward, purpose in every step. Topping the rise, she looked about. Further than seemed possible, she saw Jessica continue her relentless march to nowhere. At least she was safe.

"Little madam. I'll give her what for when I catch her," she muttered. She had a target again and moved on with greater confidence. Her skin felt cool and damp. Town clothes gave no protection against rain like this. She'd catch cold if this continued much longer, and Jessica must be soaked through. Jess' light coat, draped over her arm, was sopping wet and would offer little cover when they did get back together.

The going was hard. The surface deteriorated as it rose higher into the hills. This was a road to nowhere. Unused, unloved and abandoned. She trudged on for what seemed like hours, slowly gaining ground on Jessica. God alone knew what time it must be. She had no watch, as she relied on the clock in the car when driving, disliking the awkwardness of jewelry on her wrist while at the wheel. At last, she was within hailing distance of her daughter. "Jessica! Jess, please stop and wait. Please?"

The younger woman paused, moved another three or four steps, and halted. She stood, shoulders slumped and body trembling, looking the way she was facing.

Lauren caught up at last. She draped the wet coat over cotton that clung to the small body like a second skin, pulled it close and fastened it over her chest to give some protection.

No use pretending it was rain on that desperate face. Those were tears. Her whole body shook with sobs of deep, deep grief.

"What? What is it, my dear, dear child?"

"I'm an idiot. I let him persuade me. Let him make me believe it would all be fine. And then he does this to me. I hate him. I hate him!"

"Jamie?"

"He's not coming back. Ever. He's found someone else. Going to marry her, after only two weeks. Can you believe it? Three years together and he does this to me. I hate him!"

What to say? How to comfort a heart broken by betrayal? He hadn't fooled only Jess. Lauren and her husband had been equally convinced. Jamie would come back from his trip abroad and he and Jess would be married. It had all been planned. All been so definite.

"Well, he doesn't deserve you, Jess." She turned her daughter around and started the long trudge back to the car. "Nothing I can say will help just now, Jessica, but we love you. Come back home and live with us until you're more settled."

"I love him, Mum."

Lauren felt the slump of defeat in the body beside her. It would be pointless to remind her how much she hated the man. She held the small hand, walked with her up and down the hills, knowing that nothing she said, no words, would have the slightest effect on the situation, and may even make it worse, but silence was a weight too heavy to bear.

"It will pass. It'll take time, but it will pass. I promise you."

"Will it?"

The car was in sight. A hint of brightness patched the sky beyond. Lauren knew her daughter well. There would be no further outbursts. Just one violent expression of emotion, and then back to what passed for normality. She was a strong-willed, independent soul.

Lauren helped her into the passenger seat, taking her soaked coat and dropping it in the back. It was then she noticed the map book, on the floor between the front and back seats. She handed it to Jessica, and shed her own coat.

For a while, they sat with the heater fan blowing hot air to clear the condensation. Calm again, Jessica studied the map, and then glanced at her wristwatch. "I know where we are. If we get a shift on, we can still make it."

Better not to ask if she was certain. "Left or right?"

Jessica pointed to the road opposite the minor one they'd walked. "Drive fast, Mum. I'm not missing that plane. Not now. I'm done with him. I'll show him. He'll be sorry he betrayed me when he hears how I've done Australia on my own. He'll spend the rest of his life wishing he'd made the right choice. Get me to that airport."

Lauren shifted through the gears and risked deep puddles, as she pursued her daughter's happiness along the new route. Above, clouds slowly dispersed.

BIO: Stuart Aken is a novelist and short story writer who likes to entertain and enthrall, first and foremost. There are messages lying as undercurrents to his tales, for those who wish to discover them, but the story comes first. His short stories have won first, second, and third prizes in UK's major writing magazine, *Writers' Forum*.

His first novel, *Breaking Faith*, is a romantic thriller set in a beautiful region of England known as the Yorkshire Dales, a place he lived for a while. His science fiction digital novelette, *The Methuselah Strain*, has been picked up by his publisher and is due to be released before Christmas, 2014.

Other works include *A Seared Sky*, *Joinings, Partings,* and *Convergence.*

Enjoy more of his writing via his blog: **http://stuartaken.blogspot.com.**

The True Riches

by David E. Navarro
Award Winning Guest Author

He failed the test again. The other boys would laugh and mock. He sat watching the orange orb of the sun waver in the heat of the horizon as it slowly dipped from view.

"Salamander," the words of his mentor broke the silence. "I would like to share a story with you," the elderly white haired Curate said, waving Salamander over to him where he sat twenty feet away under a sycamore tree, reading a book of ancient poetry.

"Yes, sir," Salamander said as he rose. On his way up, he wiped his cheeks and sucked in a deep breath of mountain air to cleanse his lungs and fight back emotions. He sat next to the Curate, attentive, ready to listen.

"A child not much different than you volunteered to work in the river gardens, tending plants, pulling weeds, cleaning stone paths, and pruning wild branches."

"What was his name, sir?"

"Patience, Salamander, learn to listen and not interrupt until it is your time to speak. Do not be eager to show others you are smart. Even the fool is counted wise that keeps his mouth shut."

Salamander wanted to say *yes sir*, but chose

instead to immediately obey his mentor and remain silent, staring up into his silvery eyes. He detected a faint smile in the Curate's face.

"Well done, Salamander, you chose the wise path." He looked away and prepared to continue his story. A flock of ten swallows dove out of the tree above, playing, twisting, fluttering, and away they went into the sky.

"So the child was busy in the garden, enjoying the solitude and beauty when he came across a stone arch in the garden, two pillars on either side of the path with an arched top and flowering ivy climbing up and down." The Venerable Delwer lifted his hands over his head and back to his lap three times. "And over the top," he said waving his hand in a wide arch, "and hanging down," he cupped his hand upward as if cupping a bunch of grapes, "the arch of granite was finely carved with elaborate pictures in bas relief." Master Delwer continued, "And the child, admiring its beauty, ran his fingers in the grooves of a chariot that was carrying some sort of chest, like a treasure chest."

Salamander immersed himself into the story and pictured himself as this child. He could see and feel that stone arch and see the chariot Delwer described.

"Lost in thought, the child moved his fingers about in several grooves at once and felt the stone under his middle finger click like a tiny switch. To his great amazement and surprise, the base of the arch swung open, and in the center of the revealed hollow was a scroll case."

Salamander's eyes were wide with wonder, the sun had almost fully set, and other boys in their duties were lighting nighttime path torches nearby. None dared upset the Master teaching his student.

The Master continued. "The boy quickly looked around to see who was watching, but he was alone in the garden. Seizing the moment, he took hold of the scroll case, pulled it quickly from its hollow and backed away in case anything else was about to happen with the arch. Only the chirps of birds filled his ears.

"You can imagine his excitement as he twisted the cap loose, removed it, and saw an old rolled parchment inside with a dark purple ribbon tied about it. He dumped that scroll into his hand and with the very tips of his forefinger and thumb, he tugged on the hanging edge of the ribbon just enough to pull the knot free. He opened the scroll and read:

He who finds this scroll is chosen to complete a special mission to acquire true riches buried in a chest, in the location indicated on the map below by the symbol seen, third stone up, west column, facing north. You must follow the list below precisely:

1. Take a pickaxe, spade shovel, rope of at least twenty feet, and a hooked wheel pulley
2. Take provisions for one person and one pack animal for three days
3. Bedding and a tinder box and a few torches
4. A lodestone, needle, cork and small glass dish three inches wide and one inch deep
5. Take a pack animal with sacks to carry your

treasure

6. Such clothes as are needed and other small effects of necessity

7. You must first acquire a key in the canyon of the sun

8. You must then find instructions on the hill of the holy

9. You must follow those instructions from there

"He was quite puzzled, as you might imagine, but also thrilled with the potential of what lay before him; a real treasure map."

Master Delwer paused to sip from his water skin. The night air was getting chill. Salamander took the cue and drank from his own canteen as well. He wanted to say something to show the Curate he was listening attentively, but calling to mind the earlier lesson, he stayed his lips and waited patiently for the man to continue.

"What would be the first thing you would do?" Delwer asked.

Salamander thought a moment and then deliberately spoke. "I would go to the west column and find its northern face and count the third stone up to see what the symbol was?"

"Very good, you are listening attentively, but did the scroll say the north face or facing north? And who did it mean was facing north? The child or the column?"

"Well, that's not fair, sir," Salamander said with a twinge in his voice. "How can I know for certain what is meant by the scroll if it is not clear?"

"Life is often not fair, Salamander, and faced

with opportunity we must do the best we know to do, make a decision and move on. The worst decision ever made is no decision. Always face every challenge and every opportunity with thoughtful reflection and then make a choice."

Salamander felt it was okay to speak and said, "What did the boy choose to do, sir?"

The Curate smiled, his head nodding slightly. "The boy, after thoughtful reflection, decided to do both and to draw each symbol on his map and then to wait to see if it would become clear in the subsequent instructions."

The Venerable Delwer went on with the story, telling how the boy studied the map, and studied in the library researching place names and symbols, and gathered all the materials for his quest. His schoolmates were generally excited for him, but some were tentative and worried and asked if he thought it a dangerous undertaking. Could he really get it done in three days, and be back to school the fourth day on time? Should he take hunting tools or weapons to protect himself? What disasters might await him? To which the boy simply answered, "I have a list and a map. What could possibly go wrong?"

"Everything!" one of the boys said. "You never know what is out there, the dangers of the environment and wild beasts and foul creatures of the night. The mountain wilderness is no place for a fifteen-year old."

It was common, in that day, for a fifteen-year old to have been on several wilderness trips with his father or his clan, but never to go alone until at least thirty years of age, and even after then, to avoid it unless absolutely necessary. But the instructions clearly said to take provisions for three days for one person and the boy was intent on following the instructions precisely as the scroll had said. He was confident he would come to no harm since he had the scroll and he was the chosen one. What ill could befall a chosen one?

One of Master Delwer's attendants had quietly built a fire in a brass basin set in the ground near the tree. The flames were of significant size to radiate heat toward them, and that would increase as the embers piled up in the fire. The light was also welcome as twilight waned into the darkness of full-fledged night. The moon rose low in the east and would soon shine brilliantly in the cloudless sky, illuminating the mountainside in soft pale swaths through the trees.

Master Delwer continued the story and told Salamander how the boy set out on his journey early one morning with a trusty mule and all the provisions listed in the scroll. He had learned that sunrays on the map shone on a river that lay between mountains, and hidden lines appeared similar to a bar of music that showed "C-flat major." This was a *key* in music. He figured the space between the mountains was the canyon of the sun and the music symbol was where he would find the key.

It took him half a day to get there, and he found the deeply gouged canyon easily enough. As he hiked along the stony riverbed, he saw rock formations that resembled those drawn on the map, so he knew he was going in the right direction and kept moving toward the symbol of the music key. He sought a clue where he thought there should be one and, not knowing what to do, finally sat on a nice smooth boulder at the edge of the river and ate.

It was while he was at rest, eating and praying, that he looked up and noticed the side of the escarpment carved by the waters of ages past resembled the shape of a harp. It was partly inset in the cliff and angled in such a way that the base of the harp distinctly pointed to a peculiar pile of boulders underneath an overhang. Upon closer investigation, he found that one of the precisely placed boulders had the key of "C-flat major" etched in its side. This boulder featured an eight-inch wide crater full of dirt with several plants growing from it. He dug into the dirt with his hands and found the crater to be a far deeper and larger hole than it seemed. A foot and a half deep into the boulder, past his elbow, he felt something cold, like metal, hard and elongated. By feel, he immediately discerned it was a large skeleton key, larger and thicker than any he'd ever held, and quite heavy. He rinsed it in the river to find it was clean, shiny and hadn't corroded a bit. He wondered what kind of silvery metal this must be.

Written on the side of the key were the words, "Safe cave half way under chimney." He found the holy hill on the map one night when studying at his desk. It had eluded him for weeks, but as he sat back, exasperated from his fruitless search, the candlelight shone from behind the map and a distinct image of a descending dove of flames appeared in a watermark on a low, smooth hill at the end of the canyon.

Halfway there, night began to fall and he found the rock formation known as the chimney, and sure enough, there was a very safe cave under a dugout in the escarpment. It was difficult to get the mule to go up and in, but with persistence he managed. Using his equipment, he built a nice fire in the cave under a chute that disappeared overhead so that the smoke escaped the cave.

Next morning he came to the holy hill within a couple hours and roamed around in what appeared to be the ruins of an old refuge or maybe even a holy place. It seemed, by the precise placement of the trees and their unusual variety that a garden had been there at one time. Finally, under some thick ivy, he discovered another garden arch like the one he found when he obtained the scroll. This archway had only one side carved and it was the north side. He cleared away enough ivy to find the same chariot that was on the original arch and fingered it in the same way until the base of this arch opened and he found another scroll. The meaning of the second scroll was a mystery. It only had a bunch of letters on it, all over the front and back. He then noted the symbol on the western column of the arch, north face, three stones up, and found it to be a perfect match for a symbol on the map, a few hours from where he stood.

He arrived there in good order after eating and tending to the mule. He inspected the area, which had an outcropping of rock, and all over the rocks were etched symbols. Other nearby protruding rocks also had symbols, but eventually he found a flat face with the symbol from the map and began to dig in the ground in front of it. Using the pickaxe and shovel, he dug three feet deep and came to the top of the chest. He cleared around it, but it was too heavy to lift. The boy hung a pulley from a tree, tied the rope to the chest, and used the mule to pull the chest out of the earth.

He tried to insert the key into the hole, but it was too large, and the chest only appeared to be made of wood. It was actually carved stone, which explained why it was so heavy. Not giving up, he inspected the stone chest and found words were etched into the back of it. He cleared away the dirt until he could read the message.

Your heart may be as heavy as this chest when you realize that there are no gems, no jewels, no precious metals here. But faint not. The journey was to teach you about the true riches in life which are not silver and gold, but wisdom and knowledge of the holy, and a single eye that is flooded with light in spiritual understanding of life and the universe. The key to the true riches is in your own hands – what choices you will make, where you will go, and what you will do when you discover what you have. Take the needle and rub it with the lodestone. Pour water in the dish, balance the needle on a piece of cork in the water and let it point you north. Leave the chest but take everything else you have with you; follow the needle until night and find shelter. In the day, follow it again back to the garden from whence you came and ponder the things you have acquired on this journey.

"How do you think the boy felt?" Master Delwer asked him.

"I don't know," Salamander said. "I suppose he felt let down unless he learned something great that led to the true riches."

"Oh, he learned many things about himself on his journey… his own confidence alone in the wilderness, his ability to puzzle out the map and situations to find what he was seeking, and how persistence paid off time and again. But the real learning came when he was sitting back in that garden thinking about the whole journey and considering the disappointment of the stone chest. He cheered himself up with the things he had learned, and was proud to have successfully completed a quest in the mountains by himself.

"But it was the second scroll that he found himself staring at, trying to figure out what the letters A-K-L-C-U-E-Y-T-M-R-I-K-N-P-T-I meant. Slowly it came to him when he noticed the word *trick* in those letters, and soon after, the letters for *key* became clear, a "trick key." But what did the other letters mean? In the next minute, he realized that the whole puzzle spelled out *trick platinum key.* The key was solid platinum. With the size and weight of it, he had the key to the treasure in his hand ever since he found it in the stone."

Salamander shook his head. Several pops in the fire sent sparks hurtling into the air. Master Delwer paused, as though waiting for him to say something.

"So, sir, he learned not to rush to conclusions then?" Salamander's cheeks lifted and his eyes curled, like his face just shrugged its shoulders, unsure of his answer.

"No, but you just did," Master Delwer laughed and then calmly proceeded to say, "What he learned, Salamander, is that sometimes the key to your success is already in your hand, and if you are distracted and focused on other things, you will miss it and do extra work and bear unnecessary burdens. You will pass the Acolyte's test next time if you realize you already have what it takes to succeed."

"Thank you, Master," Salamander said as he sat upright, feeling much better. "Was that a true story?"

"I'll take you to that stone chest and show it to you someday."

"You know where it is?"

"Of course I do, Salamander. That child was me."

BIO: David E. Navarro was born in Newport, Rhode Island, grew up in inner city Chicago, and moved to Indiana until college. His love of poetry and writing began at age eight. In 1980, he was a featured poet in the *Purdue Exponent.* Since then his articles, essays, short stories and poems have appeared in various magazines, publications, literary journals, anthologies, and online. He compiled and produced the poetry anthology, *Between Life and*

Language in 2009, and *Dare to Soar* in 2013, a diverse collection of his own poems. Navarro lives in the Greater Los Angeles area. Learn more about him at **http://www.de-navarro.com.**

Double Rescue

by Joyce Brennan
Award Winning Guest Author

Shelby's car hit a patch of black ice, fishtailed to the right and then spun wildly around, crashing into a mailbox on the left side of the road. Her head snapped back and then struck the steering wheel. Seconds before she blacked out, she vaguely remembered the incessant blaring of the horn.

She blinked at the stranger leaning over her, holding an icepack to her throbbing head.

"You're awake."

"Where am I?" She cringed. "Who are you?"

"Take it easy. You had an accident. I'm Clint Jackman." A grin tugged at the corner of his mouth. "You sure did a job on my mailbox."

"Sorry."

"Just kidding. I didn't find any broken bones. I think you're okay except for a nasty bump on your forehead."

"Where's my car?"

"I'll haul it into the driveway as soon as the snow stops."

Shelby struggled to sit up. "You don't understand. I have to go. I didn't count on having travel trouble. I thought, *I have a list and a map. What could possibly go wrong?'* Well, now I see what could go wrong."

"Lady, you're not going anywhere in this storm. Just relax and I'll get you something to drink. Tea or Coffee?"

Shelby sank back on the sofa. "Coffee, thanks. A dash of cream, if you have any."

"Made a fresh pot of coffee. Will milk do?"

Shelby nodded and took stock of her surroundings. Dated furnishings, no knick-knacks, but a sense of comfort. Her rescuer filled two mugs, carried them to the living room and placed them on a wooden table. He eased down on a chair next to her.

"What brings you out in this weather, if you don't mind my asking?"

"It's complicated."

He grinned again. "We have all night. I don't imagine this storm will let up until morning. Now what's this about a list and a map?"

Shelby sighed. "My father died a few weeks ago. I took a leave of absence from work to settle his estate and close up the house. While sorting through his belongings, I came across a letter from Harlan Montgomery who lives in Cross Creek." She stopped and looked up. "Is Cross Creek near here?"

"Sixty or seventy miles north."

"Then I still have time to get there before Christmas."

"What about the letter?" he said.

"It's in my backpack. Did you bring it inside?"

"After I settled you on the sofa, I went back to check the car. I grabbed your backpack and laptop then locked the door. They're on the floor next to the sofa."

Shelby reached for the backpack and opened the zipper. She retrieved the letter and handed it to Clint.

He read aloud.

Dear Stephen,

Again, Clara and I thank you for your assistance. Your support has been a blessing these past two years. As you requested, attached is a wish list from the children. I'm sure you still have the map. We look forward to seeing you.

Merry Christmas,

Harlan Montgomery

"Are they relatives?" Clint asked.

"No. When I searched Dad's files, I discovered he found them through a church outreach program. His records show he's made the trip from northern California to Idaho the past three years. I printed a copy of the map to the Montgomery house from Dad's computer. Evidently Harlan and Clara Montgomery foster five children and have a difficult time making ends meet."

"And the list?"

"Gifts for the children, I guess. Dad had already purchased, wrapped and labeled everything. They're packed in the back of my car. Dad also included a list of provisions he planned to buy. I purchased the supplies before I left his house."

Clint recalled his childhood. His parent's religion didn't allow for celebrating holidays. Instead, he was required to spend long hours reading the Bible. He enlisted in the Army to escape the family's radical practices.

"I don't understand your sense of urgency. Why don't you wait a few days until the storm passes?"

Shelby glared at him. "And have the children miss out on Christmas? That's not an option."

"So you plan to carry out your father's mission."

"As soon as I can get back on the road."

Clint leaned back in his chair. "Your car doesn't seem damaged. Do you mind if I look at the map?"

She reached into the backpack and handed him the map and directions.

"Hmm."

"What?"

Lines crossed his forehead. "I'm not sure you want to go up there alone."

"What do you mean?"

"This part of Cross Creek could be snowed in."

"Nonsense," Shelby grumbled. "The children have to go to school. The roads are surely kept open."

"I suspect these kids are home schooled. Most folks in the area are ranchers."

"Well, it doesn't matter. If Dad delivered Christmas gifts the past two years, I can take over the task."

The corner of his mouth twitched as if he attempted to hold back a laugh. Shelby hadn't focused on his face, but now she took stock of her host. Tall, lanky, and incredibly handsome. His dark blue eyes seemed to penetrate her soul. She had a sudden urge to touch the small white scar running down the side of his face.

"Are you driving your father's vehicle?" Clint interrupted her musings.

"What? No, he had a truck."

"Four-wheel drive, I'm betting."

"Okay, I get your point, but don't you understand? The children are expecting Christmas gifts. I can't disappoint them. Maybe I can rent a truck or…"

"Not around here."

"Exactly where am I, anyway?"

Clint pointed to an area. "We're not on the map, but this will give you an idea of the location. I'm not sure how you arrived here. You probably took a wrong turn at the last small town."

Shelby slumped back on the couch. "Is there anyone who could drive me to the Montgomery's?"

"Don't look at me. I have no desire to go out in this weather."

"Do you live here alone?"

"Just me and Gracie." Clint indicated a large shepherd sleeping in front of the fireplace. "I own the general store next to the mailbox you rammed into."

"I didn't see any lights. Is your living space part of the business?"

"These rooms are behind the store. I'm closed, but if anyone needs something in an emergency, they come around to the back and let me know."

"How do you make a living in the middle of nowhere? I mean, is there enough business to support you?"

"From the store? Not really. I bought it mostly for the living quarters, after a stint in the army. I do a little better than break-even but I keep it open for convenience. I earn my keep working for a computer company. I repair and reprogram computers remotely."

Shelby nodded her head. "I'm a visiting nurse and mostly schedule my own hours. It allows me to paint, my real passion."

"Portraits?"

"Never." She laughed. "I paint landscapes. Trees and mountains aren't critics."

Clint stood. "It's getting late. Will you be okay on the sofa for the night?" He seemed to notice her apprehension and added, "Don't worry, you're safe."

"I'll be fine."

He brought out bedding and placed it on the chair. "Anything else?"

"The bathroom?"

Clint indicated a door off the kitchen. "I'll leave the hall light on. See you in the morning."

The aroma of coffee and crackling of bacon woke her out of a sound sleep. She took a minute to orient herself, remembering the accident.

"How are you feeling?" Clint called from the kitchen.

"Okay. Maybe a little stiff."

"Car crashes will do that. How do you like your eggs?"

"Over easy." Shelby sat up and stretched. "I could use a shower."

"If you can wait, breakfast is ready."

She slipped on her shoes, padded out to the kitchen, and sat at the table.

Clint filled a plate and slid it over to her. "Hot sauce or ketchup?"

"Just cream for my coffee."

He sat a carton of milk in front of her.

"Now, about my trip. Won't you reconsider and drive me there? I'll be glad to pay you."

His face tightened. "The last thing I want to do is drive further north in a blizzard."

Shelby glanced out the kitchen window. "It's stopped snowing. Think of those five little children waiting for Santa's visit. How about I rent your truck?"

"No way. It's big and bulky, not like your little match-box car."

"I get good mileage on my compact car," Shelby sniffed.

"A lot of good it does when you plow into a mailbox."

"Oh, that's what this is about. You're sore because I ruined your mailbox. I'll pay for the damage. Never mind. You said my car wasn't harmed. I'll be on my way."

"You can't be serious. You could run into snowdrifts deep enough to bury your car. You might not be found until the spring thaw."

"Regardless, I'm going to give it my best shot." She took her plate and cup to the sink. "If you don't mind, I'll take a shower and then I'll get going."

Clint watched his houseguest strut toward the bathroom. For a wisp of a woman, less than 5'4", she had grit. Obviously, she was determined to deliver the packages to the family in Cross Creek, no matter what he said. He reached for the phone and called the Idaho weather bureau. After listening to the report, he paced the kitchen. No way was he going to allow this headstrong but misguided lady to take off by herself. While she showered, he towed her car into the driveway and transferred her cartons to the camper-shell attached to his truck. By the time he finished, she stood inside the doorway.

"What do you think you're doing?" she snapped.

"I've decided to drive you to Cross Creek to play Santa."

"But you said…"

"I know what I said, but I also listened to the weather report. There's no way you'll make the trip in that puddle-jumper. Why don't you brew another pot of coffee? You'll find thermos bottles on a shelf above the stove. Maybe you can make a few sandwiches, and I believe I have apples in the fridge. I'll pack sleeping bags and emergency supplies."

She started to reply, but he held up his hand. "I'm doing this under protest."

An hour later, they pulled out of the driveway

with Gracie seated between them.

The usual hour trip to Cross Creek took more than five. Although the snow ceased, Clint made many stops to check drifts covering parts of the road. Fortunately, his four-wheel-drive truck plowed through the white-powder drifts. After Shelby misread the map and missed a turn, he had to backtrack. Clint fought the knot growing in his stomach, but clamped his lips to keep from criticizing, not wanting to up the tension.

"I would have never made it," Shelby confessed. "I appreciate your driving me." She filled a travel mug with coffee and handed it to him.

"Thanks, but we're not there yet. Check the map. There should be a turn-off ahead, unless we missed it. We've traveled about sixty miles, if that will help."

"According to Dad's directions, we should turn right immediately after we cross a small bridge. A long dirt road leads to the Montgomery house."

Clint smiled at her use of the word *we,* as if he was an eager supporter of her cause. He turned his attention back to the road when his truck skidded to the side on the ice-covered steel bridge. He regained control and pulled onto the lane, glad to see house lights flickering ahead. "Looks like the ranch," he said.

"Aren't you excited? I can't wait to meet the family."

Clint grunted. The only thing on his mind was the long trek home. Although he'd never been around children, he trusted the Montgomery's would put them up for the night. He certainly didn't want to start back after dark. He glanced at his traveling companion. Gracie sat on the edge of the seat. He hoped the Montgomery family would appreciate her enthusiasm.

As they approached the house, the front door of the clapboard ranch flew open. Before Clint could stop the truck, three young children raced toward them. A woman stood in the doorway holding another child, while a toddler held onto her skirt.

Clint's German Shepherd perked up her ears when Shelby climbed out of the truck and introduced herself and Clint. Once inside, Shelby explained why she had taken over her father's mission.

"I'm so sorry about your father," Clara said. "When we didn't hear from him, we figured he couldn't make the trip this year." She introduced the children while Gracie tolerated their pets and hugs.

"Where's Mr. Montgomery?"

"He's out at the barn, doing chores. Now, you two rest. Help yourself to coffee and I'll get back to cooking." Clara turned abruptly when she heard a crash. "Here, take the baby while I see what's going on." She thrust the small child into Clint's arms.

His mouth flew open. He held the baby girl at arm's length, afraid he'd crush her. He searched for Shelby, but she had followed Clara to the kitchen. One of the girls who looked to be about eight or nine looked up at him with a sober expression.

"She won't break. Her name is Marilee and

she likes to be cuddled."

"Yeah?" Clint pulled the baby closer to him. "Like this?"

Before the little girl could answer, the baby reached up and touched his face. She gurgled and cooed and Clint lost his reserve.

Clara appeared and took the baby from Clint. "Sorry about that. The boys were trying to sneak into the cookie jar. Why don't you unload your truck while I put dinner on the table?"

A freckle-faced nine-year old shrugged on his parka. "My name's Billy. I can help."

Clint grinned at the eager boy. "I'd appreciate it."

Clint and Billy lugged in boxes while Shelby and the two older girls lined the cartons against the wall in the living room and toted the supplies in the kitchen. The table was set and aroma of beef stew and freshly baked biscuits drifted through the house. Harlan, back from chores, joined them and said a quick blessing before they ate.

Clint was amazed by the children's manners. They sat quietly as Harlan filled their plates and passed them around. Clara pulled the highchair next to her and fed the toddler.

"Don't plan on starting back tonight. Please spend Christmas with us," Harlan said to Clint.

"I'll take you up on your offer. It was a difficult enough trip in the daylight."

Shelby added, "It didn't help that I misread the map."

"Easy enough to do. We're in the middle of

nowhere, but it's a great place for the kids."

"Don't they get lonely?" Shelby asked.

Billy spoke up. "We don't have time. Mom and Dad keep us busy with schoolwork, chores and all, and we play games every night. Monopoly is my favorite."

"I like Crazy-Eights best," one of the girls added.

After they finished dessert, Shelby stood to help clear the table. Clara placed her hand on Shelby's arm. "Each child has a job. Tonight, Betty and Joanne are on kitchen duty. I know you must be exhausted. I'll show you where to sleep. We'll all get up early to see what Santa brought."

Shelby shared a bedroom with the two oldest girls. Clint rolled out his sleeping bag in the boy's room.

Bright sunlight awoke Shelby early Christmas morning.

Billy shook Clint. "Quick, get up. Mama said Santa came last night."

Clint tried to orient himself as Billy tugged at his arm. "Hurry, we can't open anything until everyone is downstairs."

Clara met Clint at the bottom of the stairs holding a mug of coffee. "Is black okay?"

He smiled. "Perfect." He followed her into the living room. Four eager faces impatiently waited for everyone to find a seat. Shelby held the baby while Clara handed out the presents. Clint had never witnessed a Christmas celebration. The children whooped with delight as they open the presents

Shelby's father had purchased.

"Just what I wanted," Billy held up a building set.

There were books, dolls, metal cars and trucks, and everything the children had asked for. Add to that, a stocking filled with small toys and treats for each child. Clint squeezed back a tear that threatened to escape. Shelby reached over and took his hand.

"Worth the trip?"

"I'm converted. I never saw anything like this. Look at their faces."

"I hope you know how much we appreciate this. We would have had little to give the children this year," Clara said.

Shelby handed the baby to Clint and unpacked the last carton, marked *personal.* "These are gifts for you and Harlan."

Clara's face took on color. "We didn't expect this. The food he sent was more than enough." She unwrapped a wool sweater and matching scarf. Harlan tried on fur-lined gloves and sighed when he noticed four pairs of insulated wool socks.

"Your father knew what I needed. I don't know what to say."

"You deserve everything for sharing your home with these children," Shelby said.

"Let's have breakfast before you return. We'll let the children join us when they're ready." Clara placed the baby in a crib and led them to the kitchen. By nine o'clock, Shelby and Clint loaded the truck and began the trip home.

"That was an eye-opener for me," Clint said. "I never realized…"

"…the absolute joy?"

"Yeah. The children's faces told the story. And the baby! I've never held a baby before. I'm glad you talked me into driving you."

"Harlan and Clara invited us to return this summer."

"You going?" he said.

"If you'll go with me."

Clint reached over and took her hand. "I wouldn't miss it. Merry Christmas, Shelby."

BIO: Joyce has been published in four anthologies, and has written seven novels. She currently writes romance and romantic suspense for Tirgearr Publishing. Her latest eBooks, *Misplaced* and *The Hidden Journal* are available on Amazon. Joyce resides in Las Vegas, Nevada, with her husband, Tom. Visit her blog at **www.joycebrennan.blogspot.com.**

The Break

by Kara Donadt
Award Winning Guest Author

I've heard that opposites attract, which may explain why I'm friends with Mandi. She's a petite redhead who's slightly younger than I and tackles the world with the ferocity of a tigress, whereas I, on the other hand, am not petite and am regularly tackled *by* the world.

We met through work. Actually, she hired me to be her assistant, to fetch her coffee and do other grunt-work duties. Though I often feel more like a "Mandi Project" than her friend, I still cling to the relationship.

Last week, when I was in the coffee room on my break, Mandi blew in like a mini tornado, an aura of excitement around her.

"Good news, Dayna. I've just signed us up with the Extreme Adventurers. They're heading out to Dinosaur Provincial Park to do a scavenger hunt this weekend," she announced while she searched the fridge for leftovers.

I choked and sputtered on my tepid coffee. "What?" The idea of traversing the moonlike terrain in the dark didn't appeal to me in the slightest.

"S-sorry," I sputtered, "but I can't, I… um, told my dad I'd help him organize his garage this weekend." Which was the truth.

"You can help him the following weekend," she said.

"But I promised to take his recycles in," I tried again.

"Don't be like that," she said. "We'll have a great time!"

Mandi seized a brown paper bag from the fridge and rummaged through it. I could see the yellow sticky note that said it belonged to Paul in accounting. "You can drive," she said, as she pulled out a granola bar. It was never a question with her. Always an instruction. I stared into my mug, wishing the black liquid glistening at the bottom were an escape portal, but it wasn't.

The Extreme Adventurers are a group of twenty-somethings who meet regularly to do crazy things like skydiving, hang-gliding and whitewater rafting. This particular event was about wandering the southern Alberta Badlands in the dark and then partying afterwards. I was pretty sure the "partying afterwards" interested Mandi the most as I had never known her to pass up an opportunity to go carousing.

The Badlands wilderness is hard enough to negotiate in the daytime, let alone at night. I could only imagine how treacherous it would be in the dark, with rocky surfaces and deeply carved rills, pipes, and tunnels, where jagged crevices were carved by the prehistoric ice age and now served as hazardous drop-offs. Small spiny cacti hidden amongst the grassy fescues lay ever ready to impale a misplaced foot, not to speak of scorpions and other nocturnal creatures skittering about, just waiting to sting or bite a fool like me.

The next day, Mandi called at 4:30 to cancel because some guy she'd been waiting to date finally asked her out. I was less than happy. It wasn't the first time I'd been ditched in the name of an opportunity she couldn't pass up, and again I promised myself it would be the last.

"Oh, don't be mad," she said. "You've got nothing else on the go"—*as usual*, was the implication —"and who knows, you might even have a good time. That is, if you don't chicken out."

I hated her smugness. As I contemplated canceling, too, she added, "I hear there are going to be three guys for every girl, so you might even have a chance at finding a date." The gut-punch words sealed the deal.

"Gee, thanks, Mandi," I said, now determined to go, out of spite. "And I *can* find a date. I was married once, remember?"

"Oh, you know what I mean. Well, I've gotta run. Have fun, and try not to get lost," she said with a laugh.

I clutched the silent phone long after the disconnection, then reluctantly placed it in its cradle and heaved a heavy sigh. When I heard a light rap on my door, I muttered, "Come in." Jade, the receptionist, flitted into the room like a pixie fairy and dropped a large white envelope down onto my desk.

Written on the outside of the envelope in Mandi's tidy handwriting was my name, so I lifted the flap and peered inside. I pulled out a hand-drawn map with a scavenger list. I tucked the flap back in and then glanced up at the round white-faced clock on the wall. It read 4:50. If I had half a brain, I would leave forty minutes early. That way, I could zip home, get organized, and find a flashlight before making the hour-long drive east. But I didn't leave early and ended up being rushed.

The sun dropped behind the horizon as flat farmlands surrendered to a mighty gorge and the landscape became a strange, foreign Mars-like planet. I drove down the curvy road to the park's visitor center where I pulled in next to a group of cars that I presumed were my fellow hunters. I grabbed my gear from the back seat and headed for the meeting spot listed on the map. We were to meet at the mouth of the Coulee Viewpoint Trail at 7:30 pm; however, as luck would have it, I arrived at 8:05 to find they had already dispersed on the hunt. I was on my own.

The air was crisp and the sky clear. I muttered, "I have a list and a map. What could possibly go wrong? It's a simple scavenger hunt. Right?"

Wrong. I should have returned to my car and driven home. But, of course, I didn't.

The first thing I did was unfold the scavenger list and the map. I headed off with map in hand and a small backpack stuffed with a light fleece jacket, a flashlight, and a bottle of water. The crunch of my footsteps filled the still, fall air. As I wandered up the trail, I reasoned against a sliver of fear that it shouldn't be too difficult to catch up to the others.

They were only a half hour ahead.

The earth under my shoes shifted as I climbed the hill. In that moment, the wish to own hiking boots was quickly followed by the thought, *What the heck am I doing out here in the first place? I've never been a hiker. I'm a casual stroller who prefers verdant parkways within the city limits. It's not that I'm a couch potato. I just prefer easy.*

When sweat dampened my brow, I stopped to wipe it with the back of my hand. The elastic band in my hair loosened and gave freedom to a few random strands, so I yanked it free and refastened it.

The diminishing sunlight made it difficult to read the scrawl on the scavenger list, so I retrieved the old flashlight from my pack. It was one I inherited—or rather borrowed from dad's garage years ago when I needed to search the attic for squirrel nests. I felt a guilty pleasure in not having returned it as I attempted to read the scavenger list. When I clicked the switch, a weak yellow glow emitted from the lens. I shook it, as if that would improve the light. It didn't. I twisted the bottom cap off, dropped the batteries out and reinserted them, hopeful that my actions would improve the flashlight's performance. No such luck. Resolved to make the best of it, I held the flashlight as close to the paper as possible and squinted.

First on the list was "a cactus thorn." How hard could it be to tug a thorn from a cactus? Next was "a cottonwood leaf," "a dinosaur bone (picture)," "a cave (picture)," and "a campsite souvenir, for example: firewood or picture of a fire pit." The thought of using my ancient flip phone to snap a picture amused me. Perhaps I should've followed Mandi's advice and bought a smart phone.

When I got to the bottom of the list, it read, "Bonus! Find the hidden treasure and the group pays for your team's drinks tonight!" I wondered what the "hidden treasure" could be. If it were up to me, I'd leave a stuffed dinosaur in an outhouse. I smiled. I could tell I was beginning to relax for the first time since I got up that morning. Later, Mandi would tell me the treasure was a sixty-pounder of whiskey.

My mind wandered in step with my feet as I trudged along the path. Soon my thoughts turned to work. True, it wasn't a dream job, but it paid the bills (or so my internal argument claimed). In a different life, I would be a lawyer, and a good one, too—even better than Mandi. I guffawed and stumbled over a rock. Dusk had settled in, and with just the dim light of a dying flashlight to guide me, it was difficult to see.

When thirty minutes had passed and I still hadn't caught up with anyone from the group, I grew concerned. Being alone in the dark was anything but fun. Besides, where were all those available guys? I grimaced as Mandi's sharp words replayed in my head: *Try not to get lost.*

As I journeyed along, I came to a point where I had to climb the side of a steep hill on all fours.

When I finally reached the peak, the wind had picked up and the temperature had dropped a few degrees. Earlier, I could hear the distant howls of coyotes and occasionally, far away voices. Now I heard only the wind, and somehow I had managed to lose the main trail. I pulled out the map and unfolded it. When the wind tried to strip it from my hands, I squatted down close to the hard earth, huddled with my poor flashlight pointed at the paper. No matter how I shifted the map, it no longer made any sense to me. Worse yet, nothing matched up with anything on the map. I was officially worried.

I scanned the area for any signs of life, hoping to see a beam of light from someone's flashlight or the glow from a lantern or campfire. Nothing but black dark. The sky was bejeweled with dazzling bright stars, but there was no moon to provide illumination. Around me, dark shadows threatened the unknown while monstrous hoodoo silhouettes loomed overhead.

Did I hear footsteps? I flashed the light's faint beam in the direction of the noise, but it flickered and died. In a panic, I shook it, willing it to come back to life. When it refused, I slammed the useless thing on the hard ground and broke it to pieces.

As I squatted on my haunches, I rocked in place and choked back tears. I dug into my pocket and pulled out my cell phone. When I flipped it open, I immediately noticed I had no service. "Great," I muttered. Then I looked at the time, astonished to see it was 9:45 p.m. It suddenly dawned on me that my fellow hunters might have already left the park. Would they even know I was out there?

Vulnerable to the panic bubbling just below the surface, I began to retrace my steps, praying I was going in the right direction, and tumbled head over heels down a steep embankment that disintegrated below my feet. When my body finally came to a stop, I was lying face down with my feet higher than my head. The stabbing pain of cacti thorns quickly replaced my daze. I blindly moved my hands in search of a cactus-free place to push myself up to my knees. Gingerly, I peeled off my backpack and set it beside me. Careful not to push the thorns farther into my palms, I searched the pouches for a tissue. Nothing.

"This is so my life," I spat. Warm tears streaked down my cheeks. With great effort, I lifted my aching body upright, and instantly lost my footing on the edge of a crevice. Down I went, rolling and plummeting into a deep hole, landing with a hard thud. "Oomph" went the air from my lungs. Then a peculiar blackness enveloped me, blotting out the stars that twinkled in the inky sky above me, and the world as I knew it disappeared.

At one point, when I broke through the oblivion, I was acutely aware of how much trouble I was in.

Looks like you've got yourself into another hole, dear, echoed my dead mother's voice. The pain in my head was excruciating. An incessant pounding hammered in my skull and made my stomach retch. Slowly, I turned my head to the side and let the vomit dribble out. I tried to push up onto my elbows. The attempt was met with unbearable pain that sent a high-pitched shock throughout my body.

I can't do this anymore. Why do I always make bad choices? I should've gone to college. Why did I stay in a bad marriage for so long or waste all of my savings on a fraudulent investment? I'm tired of hurting … of being a failure. I fell down and drifted into the abyss.

I don't know how long I lay there, but voices and yelling brought me back to life. The sky was blue-pink now. I tried to push myself up, but was stopped again by the searing pain. When I tried to call out, my voice was no louder than a squeak. *Please find me*, I prayed.

It seemed like an eternity until I saw two beautiful faces peer over the edge of the crevice.

One face looked away and yelled, "We found her!" and the other looked at me and said in a soothing tone, "We're here. You're safe."

When I finally returned to work, hobbling around in a toe-to-thigh cast, I was no longer satisfied with keeping the status quo. I guess that's what happens when you're able to slip past death's doorstep unseen. One morning, I stood in front of the file cabinet, one hand filled with papers and the other on a crutch. I struggled to pull the drawer open. It wasn't that I couldn't. It was just that I no longer wanted to, so I gave Mandi my two weeks' notice.

Mandi agreed to meet me for lunch after my doctor's appointment, when my leg cast was removed. It had been a while since we had seen each other, and I got the feeling she was avoiding me—or was it the other way around? We greeted each other with a casual hug and the usual "How's it going?" before sitting down.

"Well, you're finally looking good," Mandi said.

"Gee, thanks, Mandi. What can I say? Removing a plaster cast does nothing but improve a girl." A twinge of resentment nibbled at my core. "Where have you been? You didn't return my calls."

"Busy," she said at the same time a waitress brought two glasses of water to our table. "Heard you were accepted into law school. Congrats."

"Yes, I was." I eyed her for a moment. "To be honest, I'm a little nervous about the whole thing. Actually, a lot nervous," I said with a half-hearted laugh.

"Yeah, I would be, too, if I were you."

"What's that supposed to mean?"

"Ah, c'mon, you know. It's not like you're a super brain or anything. How's living with your dad? Are you ready to kill yourself yet?" she chuckled.

"Actually, Dad is great. Moving in with him was the best thing I've done since the Badlands accident," I said, acknowledging to myself that it was the first of a few good moves. Then I looked at Mandi, and for the first time I could see her clearly. She was stuck—in life, and on herself—and she wanted me to be stuck, too.

Mandi raised her arm to signal the waitress. "You ready to order?" she said.

"Actually, something's come up and I have to go."

"What? No lunch? Something wrong with you?" she said in an annoyed tone.

"No, Mandi, there's nothing wrong with me. In fact, I'm good. Really good." I slowly raised myself from the chair and walked away.

BIO: Kara Donadt lives in Spruce Grove, Alberta, where she writes from her home office. Each success, no matter how small, brings with it the encouragement for her to continue to write. Kara was runner up (three times) in The Saturday Serial Thriller contest and a Grab Bag winner in the 24 Hour Writing contest. Her short story, *Nancy and Her Stupid Brownies,* was published in Prairie Dog Publishing's anthology, and the story entitled **10:03** won first place in the Writer's Digest 83rd Annual Contest for Mainstream/Literary Fiction.

By Any Other Name

by Maxine Bulechek
Finalist 2014 Short Story Contest

Jim Barker relaxed into the sagging seat of a lawn chair and sipped cold beer. He ignored the people around him, his attention on fireflies sparkling over a nearby cornfield. Random musical notes competed with children's laughter as musicians tuned guitars and fiddles in the park pavilion. His sons, Keith and Ryan, greeted the other children as instant friends when they arrived. His wife, Susan, conversed with a woman who sat nearby on a quilt. At a child's sudden shriek, Jim sat forward, sharply alert.

"A blue bug! A blue bug!" Jim felt his stomach unfurl as he eased out of the chair. There was no actual distress in that cry. He winked at Susan, handed her the sweating beer bottle and went to check on the children. A scary blue bug? Interesting.

Three-year old Keith was knee-high in grass, bending over a large upturned rock. Six-year old Ryan, more cautious, watched. The instant friends observed from a greater distance. One small girl ran in circles around the group repeating her excited, or terrified, bug chant.

"You found a blue bug?" Jim asked, one of his eyebrows elevated.

"Keith did. Under the rock." Ryan pointed at

the tiny round ball.

"Yup," said Jim. "We called them roly-polys or stink bugs when I was little. They don't bite people. Here, hold one." Jim picked up a few of the BB-sized balls and gently placed one in Keith's palm, then one in Ryan's. A couple of other small hands extended. Jim placed bugs in their hands, but the circling girl stopped, with hands behind her back. "They have blue blood. When they get sick, their bodies turn bright blue. Don't touch that very bright blue one; the grayer ones are okay."

As the children stared at their palms, the bugs began to unwind, displaying seven sets of legs and two pairs of antennas.

"They aren't bugs." Ryan said. "Bugs have six legs."

"Right. Insects have three pair of legs. These have seven pair. They are technically crustaceans, related to shrimp. The mama ones carry the babies in a kangaroo type pouch. When scared, they curl into a hard ball. The part you see then is an exoskeleton. As it grows, it sheds, like a snake sheds its skin when it molts. These bugs make good pets. They live a long time, maybe five years, if you take care of them."

The children listened with rapt attention. Reverently whispered comments of "Wow" and "Ah" followed Jim's comments.

"Can we… CAN WE TAKE THEM HOME?" Keith shouted as the band began blaring the opening strains of Tom Waits' song, "Nighthawks at the Diner."

Jim nodded at his son, thinking, *Perfect music. Nighthawks are not hawks. Stink bugs are not bugs. End of lesson. Next time they can hear the scientific name and the fact that they breathe with gills. Hope that beer is still cold.*

Early the next morning, Susan placed black coffee in front of Jim. She sat across from him with a cup of herbal tea. "You look radiant," he said. "Pregnancy agrees with you."

Susan gently rubbed her protruding belly. "Keep up the sweet talk. I like hearing it, but girl or boy, this is the last one." She smiled at him. "Speaking of looking good, you look like you're applying for a job, instead of deciding who to hire."

Jim stroked the maroon silk tie centered over the buttons of his starched shirt. "For this candidate, our firm is the applicant. With his background in cancer research and vaccine development, he has his choice of employers. His leadership experience is what we need for the new division. I heard he's interviewing at John Hopkins later this week."

"You have other qualified candidates, like the one scheduled on Friday."

"Half as qualified. Today's candidate is the one we want. Be careful not to tire yourself out showing his wife around. Where are you taking her besides Amana?"

"I made a list of unique places within thirty miles, so she can choose."

"Sounds like a good plan."

"I have a list and a map. What could possibly go wrong? You said she's German?"

"So I've been told. Erika is her name. English is her fifth language. Her husband is William, *not Bill*. Marie said he was very formal when she called him about travel arrangements. His wife is probably distantly polite, too. Be your usual self. No pressure."

"If adding her husband to your staff helps develop a cancer vaccine, I can and will be cordial to the Wicked Witch of the West."

"Witch? What witch?" Ryan said as he set two plastic cups half filled with leaves next to his cereal bowl.

Little Keith followed him into the dining room, red pajamas bottoms dragging.

"There is no witch. Bugs off the table, please," Susan said.

Ryan moved one cup to the floor near his feet. "We lost one. Maybe it rolled out in the car."

Susan removed the other cup, echoing Jim's words, "Perfect pets. They could live five years." She chuckled and looked at Jim. "Don't worry. Daddy will search for it."

After pouring milk into the cereal, Susan said, "Cheryl is going to watch you today while I show a nice lady around town. Her husband might work with Daddy soon."

Susan felt an immediate rapport when she met Erika, who shared a pregnant shape. "Three more months," Susan announced. She patted her stomach and Erika smiled. After a silent minute, Susan realized Erika was plump, not pregnant. They found coinciding interests in needlework, golf, antiques and herbal tea. They laughed at the address of the fruit orchard on Berry Road, and ate lunch at a German restaurant where the chef served locally grown food. The day passed quickly.

In the late afternoon, they went to Susan's home. Susan left Erika in the dining room with the boys while she walked the babysitter to the door and paid her. When she returned, Keith was telling Erika about their evening at the park.

Erika was very quiet, and remained quiet until her husband picked her up a half-hour later. Her tone was cool when she said goodbye.

"Everything was fine when we were touring the area. Maybe she doesn't like children," Susan said. "Her entire demeanor changed after a few minutes with the boys."

"William impressed everyone. He's one of the best cancer research specialists in the world. His personality fits with the team. He could make an immediate contribution to our work. We spent the afternoon hammering out the largest employment offer we've ever made. Each partner volunteered a 2% salary reduction to fund a hiring bonus for him. I doubt there is any company that would value his work more. He'll be in tomorrow at nine."

At the appointed hour, William arrived in the conference room. He greeted the four partners and listened without displaying emotions while the employment offer was presented, then gathered his copies of the documents. He said, "I'll give you a response before the end of the month."

The partners exchanged surprised glances and

shook hands with William, unsure how to respond to his lack of enthusiasm.

Jim said, "I'll walk out with you." The two exchanged impersonal comments until they left the building. He decided to make one last effort - a Hail Mary. "William, is there something you wanted to see in this employment offer that wasn't there?"

"No. The offer is generous. If money was my only motivation, I would accept it now."

"We appreciate your dedication to this research, which is why we want you to join our staff. Yesterday you seemed interested. What has changed?"

Dr. Geiger looked at the horizon, then at Jim, weighing his words. "Where I work is only partly my choice. Erika must be happy, too. Your wife was gracious to her, but children often voice the true opinions of their parents."

Please don't say they repeated the Wicked Witch comment, Jim thought. He managed to keep his mouth from falling open while his thoughts overflowed. *How could I put that in context?*

"When your boys said their mother was driving around with a roly-poly stink bug in the car, it hurt Erika's feelings. She's not sure she'll be comfortable living here."

Jim released his breath and chuckled. He touched William's shoulder. "Let me explain." They walked to the grass on the edge of the parking lot. Jim turned over a rock, relieved to see a stinkbug on his first try. "See this?" Jim gently picked up the tightly rolled bug. "Keith and Ryan brought stink bugs home as pets last night. They lost one in the car."

William stared at Jim. "You call the noble *Armadillidium vulgare* a stink bug? Everyone knows it's a *pill-bug*."

The men laughed.

"I'll speak with Erika. I respect the research done here. It would be an honor to help develop a cancer vaccine."

After William drove away, Jim called the conference room where the partners were discussing the second-best candidate. "William is seriously considering our offer. We cleared up a little miscommunication. I need a few hours personal time. I'll be back by two."

Susan was surprised to see Jim home early. "What happened?" she asked.

The boys were hugging his legs, happy to see him. "I found out why Erika was quiet after talking to the boys yesterday." Jim sat in a leather recliner. Keith and Ryan immediately climbed on his lap, one perched on each knee.

"She thought the roly-poly stink bug in the car was a reference to her."

"Oh, no!" Susan put her hand over her mouth, then collapsed on the couch, giggling. "The poor woman. How did you explain that?"

"With the exact truth. I was grateful I didn't have to explain a wicked witch. It made me realize how much proper names matter. A nighthawk is not a hawk; a stink bug is not a bug."

"A rose by any other name..." Susan said.

"That may be, but to avoid misunderstanding, we need to say precisely what we mean. I thought we could start by teaching the boys the name for their pets."

"Mine is Sam." Ryan said.

"Your exact bug can be named Sam, but let's call them a more precise name… *Armadillidium vulgar* or Armadillo bug.

"But Daddy," Keith said, "they're not a bug."

Susan curled on her side on the couch, laughing. "Bet you wish you could explain the Wicked Witch now."

EGOT and the Pond King

by J. Lenni Dorner
Finalist 2014 Short Story Contest

"Are you sure I shouldn't take a wheelchair for my grandmother?"

"There really shouldn't be a need for one. The number for the nurse's station is on that list. Call if something comes up." The corners of the nurse's lips edge up just enough to form a polite smile. She glances at her watch.

"Right. It'll be fine. I have a list and a map. What could possibly go wrong?"

I hate the halls here. The hideous floral wallpaper peels where it meets the filthy, unending plastic rail. There are always people hanging around, grabbing that rail like it will take them away. My ears pound with the echoes of moans and sobs. I once thought no one cared enough to help the makers of the sounds. Now I've come to realize that this is a battle that can never be won, that these are the howls that come at the end. Maybe the Angel of Death has to stop for fresh air on the way here. The mingling odors of urine and disinfectant are enough to drive anyone away.

"Oscar? Is that you?"

"No, Grammy, it's Olivier. The nurse gave me a map of the grounds. She said we could go for a walk down by the pond if you like. Lunch is always better outside."

"Oh, Olivier! Yes, of course. I knew it was you. I was only teasing." She wraps her arm around mine. The softness of her skin amazes me every time. "So tell me how you have been, dear."

"I've been well, Grammy. How about you? Any new adventures?"

"Life is an adventure, Olivier. We must make the best of each day." She takes stock of our surroundings. "Even in a place like this. Let me see that map, please."

I hand it to her, along with the list of emergency information. We head toward the doors and wait for them to unlock.

"There now, that's better. If this were a treasure map, that building would be one of the obstacles meant to deter hunters," she says.

"What sort of treasure would be at the end?"

"You tell me, Oscar."

"Olivier."

"Of course, dear." Grammy veers off the paved path, heading toward a forsythia bush. She sniffs the flowers before plucking two.

"A trident. I want the treasure to be a trident from the king of the pond," I say.

She smiles at me. "That's a lovely treasure. Does it have powers?"

"Of course it does! It turns the clouds into dolphins. Special dolphins that can move on the land, swim in the water, or fly through the air. And they all obey the holder of the trident."

We near the hill that leads down to the pond. I

pull her back to the paved path. It's safer there. She lets out a soft sigh but obliges my lead. A current of air moves around us, lowering the temperature to the perfect degree. The soft blades of emeralds under our feet were cut two days ago. The sprinkling of rain this morning washed the clippings away, leaving the lawn as soft as a down comfort. Grammy insists on spreading out the picnic blanket anyway.

"There is blueberry birch in these cups," she says after taking a sip through her straw.

I nod. My hands are busy with a bag of kettle-cooked potato chips. The crunch frightens a robin away. "Tell me about how you met Grandpa."

"Of course. I was working as a waitress, hoping to save enough money to go on a trip. I wasn't sure where I wanted to go; I only knew that I wanted to fly. A young man with dark hair came in and sat at one of my tables. Every day for a month he'd show up and watch me for an hour."

"He ordered a sweet Lebanon bologna with provolone sandwich, right?"

"Yes. On buttered white bread, with the crusts cut off the bottom and sides, but not off the top."

"And you didn't take it to him." I crunch another chip, bathing my tongue in the salty goodness.

"No, I did not. I had no idea what he meant! I brought him a regular bologna with American cheese sandwich, which he refused to eat. But he always paid his bill in full and left me a generous tip." Grammy twirls the yellow flowers she had plucked between her fingers. The smile on her lips outshines the sun.

"Go on. Tell me what happened next."

"He stopped coming in for a while. I thought it was because he didn't get what he ordered. But I planned ahead, in case he did come back."

"And then?"

"Well, I had been saving up to take a trip. I finally had enough money for a flight to Philadelphia. My two-week notice was put in. The boss said I didn't need to quit just to go on vacation."

"He didn't know you weren't planning on going back."

"No, he didn't know that. People don't usually fly away and start a new life wherever they land." She pulls two sandwiches from our lunch bag and passes one to me. The parchment paper gets unfolded just a bit before she takes a long whiff. "This ground isn't terribly comfortable. How about if we walk by the water while we eat these?"

"Sure. As long as you finish the story."

She smiles and nods. I help her to her feet. The breeze isn't strong enough to take our blanket, so I leave it behind for now.

"I got to the airport early. I was so eager to fly! My plane wasn't at the gate yet, but I didn't care. While waiting in the terminal chairs, I saw the pilot and co-pilot coming. Like a fool, I waved a frantic hello, greeting them like they were celebrities. As they came closer, I recognized my customer with the funny order."

"What if you hadn't been there early that day? What if you were one of those people who rush to catch a flight at the last possible minute?"

"Oh dear, that would be regretful. Though I think we still would have found each other. Destiny is like that." Grammy smiles and takes a bite of her sandwich. "I marched over to him and said hello."

"And he said hello back. He called you Emmy."

"That's right. He knew my name from the tag I wore as a waitress. I looked at his uniform and read his name aloud."

"A. Ward," I supply with a laugh.

Grammy doubles over in a fit of giggles. "And he asked if I'd like to win him! That silly coot. Then I asked him what his full name was."

I pick up a stone and skip it across the pond. "Anthony Adam Ward," I say as my stone kerplunks under the water.

"Well, quick as a whip, I replied to him that I was going to Philadelphia, not to Broadway in New York City, so I couldn't be eligible for a Tony A. Ward. That's when he got this huge grin on his face. He asked if my middle name was Amy."

"And you had no idea why he was asking." I take a bite of my sandwich before skipping another stone.

"Nope, none at all. I informed him that it was not Amy, as a matter of fact, it was Angel. Then I reached into my purse."

One more stone skips along the water, knocking on the pond king's door. "And he told you that he didn't need to see your identification, that you didn't need to prove your name."

"Right again."

"But you weren't reaching for your ID."

"Nope. I pulled out a packet of sugar and a toothpick with a little cardboard flag."

"Which you made all by yourself, because you couldn't find a miniature flag of the country of Lebanon," I say while watching another stone zip along the water.

"That's right. Mind that you don't get dirt in your food, dear. A bird seems to have dirtied a few of the stones."

"Yes, Grammy. Finish the story."

"Oh, for sure! I handed him the little flag and sugar packet. He looked at me queer. I told him that I had been carrying them around in case I saw him while I was still a waitress. He asked why I thought he'd want such a thing. Dumbfounded, I replied that if he put the sugar on his bologna, it would be sweet. And if he planted the flag into the bread, once three quarters of the crusts were removed, of course, he could claim the sandwich was Lebanese."

We both laugh. I take another bite before skipping yet another stone. The pond king is a very heavy sleeper.

"And that's when he dropped to one knee. Right there, in the middle of the airport, causing a bunch of folks to interrupt their travels and turn our way. I never had so many eyes on me before! It looked like two gala apples were growing on either side of my nose."

I grab a larger stone and give it a good toss. It doesn't skip very far though. Perhaps lighter would be better.

"He said that he would take me to Lebanon County, which isn't far from Philadelphia. There, I could meet his family and his preacher. I asked why I would want to do that. He replied it was because he wanted to marry me. He asked me to be his Emmy A. Ward."

"And you said yes," I pick up a flat square stone and run my thumb over it.

"Well, to be honest, the first thing I said was that I never thought anyone would propose marriage thanks to a pack of sugar and a cardboard flag."

I laugh as I bend my wrist to flick the stone into the water.

"Oh, dear. Here, you can eat the rest of mine," Grammy says, stopping my hand just before I take a bite of stone. The rest of my sandwich lingers on the pond, waiting for the king to enjoy my mistake.

"He should at least let me see his trident!" I say.

"Who?"

"The pond king! Our map led us here. What does the list say? Does it mention how to wake him up?"

"Oscar Anthony Ward, you know fully right well that there is no pond king and no trident. It was only a story you made up!" Grammy says in a fret.

I make a face at the water. "Stupid pond king!

Just share the trident for a minute. Just make me one dolphin so I can ride it out of here."

"Oscar, look at me. The key to getting out of here is in your own mind, not in the pond. Come on, we'll take you back inside."

"I told you, I'm Olivier!"

Read to Me

by Joan Bassington-French
Finalist 2014 Short Story Contest

The library was asleep, or at least dozing.
Unlike during the school year, when the library
vibrated with muffled activity and each long row of
shelves ripe with the wisdom and knowledge of
academics basked in the fluorescent lighting
overhead, the summertime library lay like a vast,
slumbering colossus. The main decimal shelves
stood in silent darkness waiting for the end of
August. I could almost feel the pain of the acres of
books calling out to be perused as I walked from
the dimly lit fiction section down to the checkout
desk on the main floor. The university library
seemed so desolate and forgotten in the summer. I
felt like a heartless harpy for being there instead of
leaving the library to its sacred rest and reverently
approaching it again when school started in August.

Of course, being addicted to words as I am, I
had to skulk into the library several times a week
and raid the shelves of the open fiction section. It
called me, that crypt that was the library. I was stuck
on campus for the summer, working a job to pay
for my school bill. Reading was the cheapest form
of entertainment, and most likely the most
rewarding.

I always left the library with the relief one feels

when one has left a beloved family member's house. It was good to breathe the fresh, piney air. I love books, which the healthy stack in my arms clearly stated, but a sleeping library is a heavy place in which to be. The sky had clouded over since I had entered the library, and a refreshing wind took the place of the muggy summer heat that had lain over everything for so long. I smelled rain in the air.

Then Brendon Sargent ran up the sidewalk toward me, and any residual library ambiance still clinging to my person fled at his face. This ten-year old, the son of one of the summer faculty, was the scourge of my life. For some reason he attacked and attached himself to me as often as possible. Today he had obviously escaped from the summer day camp on campus.

"Miss Joan, Miss Joan!" he shouted, his large, round, innocent eyes popping out at me.

"What is it, Brendon?" I sighed, wondering how it was that the densest segment of the male population always decided to attach itself to me.

"I just wanted to say hi," Brendon said with a cherubic smile, his round cheeks growing rounder as his too-large teeth stared at me menacingly.

"Hi," I said, hoping to escape this youthful pestilence. I enjoy being around children at times, but that day was simply not one of those times.

"Chocolate?" he said, proffering half a bar.

"Uh, no thanks. I just had lunch," I said, interpreting 'a solid hour ago' as 'just.' Sometimes one is forced to take poetic license for the greater good of the digestion.

"Want to read to me?" he asked

Why don't ten-year-old boys do something useful like play video games or terrorize small creatures? Why must they remember one solitary act of kindness and continually lobby for a repeat performance? And I couldn't even plead the lack of reading material; even Helen Keller could have seen the stack of literature in my arms.

"No," I said. "I don't have time today."

Brendon's face fell like an anvil, and I continued on my way with a sigh of relief. He was persistent, though. "Will you have time tomorrow?"

"Probably not." I've known mosquitoes to be less tenacious than Brendon Sargent.

At that moment, thunder rumbled and a dashing sheet of rain began pelting our unsuspecting heads. I made a mad dash for the library and was followed by Brendon. We staggered into the lobby and gasped for breath.

"That was close!" Brendan laughed, his voice springing up and out into the echoing hallway. The librarian at the checkout desk, whom I had always counted as a friend, fixed her glaring eye upon me as if somehow this was my fault. Apparently she thought Brendon was with me.

"Come on, let's go upstairs," I whispered. Things were darker and creepier upstairs, even in the fiction section. People simply didn't come to this library in the summer.

Up the winding staircase, we climbed. I envisioned sitting in one of the leather chairs and reading Agatha Christie's *Why Didn't They Ask Evans* for the fifth time. Somehow the little parasite would have to be gotten rid of, although how, I knew not.

"Will you read to me?" he asked again, when we reached the top. I sent a timely glare in his direction. I was in no mood to read to annoying little boys.

"Look, why don't you go on a treasure hunt," I said.

"Where?" he asked.

"Here." I pulled a library brochure from my book bag. I always kept one there because of the floor diagram on the back. "Here's a map of the library. Why don't you find some books? I'll write down a few titles for you." I took a pen and scratch book from my bag and jotted down such captivating titles as *The Complete Works of Keats*, *An Anthology of Middle Eastern Literature*, and *Economic Crises in Outer Mongolia*. "Can you find all of those?"

"Sure," he said. He took the list from me and scanned it with a deepening look of concern.

"Are you certain?" I asked.

"I have a list and a map. What could possibly go wrong?" he said.

Maybe it was the way he said it, but suddenly that sounded like a challenge to me.

Brendon scampered off into the deeply shadowed portion of the second floor while I betook myself to the leather chairs and read to the sound of rain and thunder.

I was on chapter four before I realized Brendon had not yet returned. "Oh, great," I muttered. A feeling akin to a screwdriver being wound into my stomach overtook me. If a librarian caught Brendon getting into trouble, I would be the one who got the blame.

"Brendon!" I called out. No one else was in the reading area, and I doubted that anyone was in the darkened area, aside from Brendon, of course. With a sigh of resignation, I plunged into the shadows to find him.

Although I called three times, he didn't answer. A split-second glare of lightning through the tall windows on the far wall made me jump. A moment later, the answering call of thunder crashed overhead and made the whole great room tremble. "Brendon?" I called out.

Suddenly he was there, leaping out at me in the darkness from behind a bookshelf. I screamed, and what a scream! I think it sounded like something between a screeching violin and a hyena on steroids. I know what doesn't kill you is supposed to make you stronger, but I think I almost passed out from that scream. I staggered back and clutched at the nearest shelf. Brendon was doubled up with laughter in front of me.

Then they came. The librarians must have thought someone was committing murder on the second floor because they rushed up with all speed. The fluorescent lights hummed to life, and in an instant we were surrounded by three ghastly-faced library workers.

Think quickly, I told myself. The gimlet-eyed librarian from the front desk looked like she was ready to thrash me. Apparently, there was no doubt as to who had done the screaming, possibly because I was blue in the face from lack of oxygen.

"There was a terrible creature," I gasped. "It leapt right out at me in the dark."

I must have sounded compelling, or perhaps they thought I meant a mouse. At any rate, the librarians suddenly lost a good deal of interest in the two of us as they went around searching for whatever had gotten into the library. They never did remember to ask why we were in the darkened area in the first place. Naturally, we didn't try to enlighten them on the subject. I simply caught Brendon's eyes, jerked my head toward the staircase, and started walking. He got the idea and followed me. Sometimes it's easier to brave an elemental storm than the wrath of a librarian, or three librarians, in our case.

We left the library and ran through the rain to the nearest unlocked edifice: the science building. Dripping water over the synthetic marble floor of the lobby, we simply looked at each other with wide eyes.

"Don't ever do that again," I said, rubbing water out of my face and grimacing as wet hair fell over my fingers.

Brendon didn't even bother to look repentant. Instead, he shook water out of his hair like a little puppy. "Now will you read to me?" he asked with a grin.

Lana's Sister

by Diane Maciejewski
Finalist 2014 Short Story Contest

Sweat trickles down my sister's dirt-smudged cheeks. "What took you so long?" she demands as she switches off the vacuum cleaner.

"I took a wrong turn."

Lana's eyes rest on my pressed jeans. "How do you do it? You moved to town three days ago. You've already hung botanical prints on your walls. And somehow you found time to iron?"

I start to speak, but she holds up a hand. "I know. 'Organization is the key to success.' Spare me."

Let it go, I think as I lay my extra house key on her dining room table. "Why the summons?"

"I need a few things for the party tonight," she says as she swipes hair out of her eyes, "but I have to finish cleaning, make potato salad, and cut up the fruit. Would you go to the grocery for me and then run over to Mrs. Klein's to pick up the brownies? Jenny prefers them to birthday cake."

"Are you forgetting I haven't lived here for thirty years like you? I don't know my way around. I have no sense of direction, and I don't know Mrs. Klein." I catch myself wringing my hands. "Besides, isn't Jenny's birthday next Saturday?"

"Daughter dearest is camping with friends

next weekend."

"But …"

"Don't worry. I placed the orders and drew a map for you." Lana locks her lake-blue eyes onto mine. "I need your help."

Point scored. Unlike my ex-boss, ex-husband, and my son in Colorado, Lana still needs me. "Give me the addresses. I'll use my phone's GPS."

"I don't know the addresses."

"What!"

She shrugs. "Who needs addresses in a small town?"

Grateful that the Upper Peninsula is considerably cooler in September than Chicago, I roll down the car windows, start the engine, and check the clock. It's just past two, and the party isn't until six. I have a list and a map. What could possibly go wrong? I'll have time to go home, shower, and change before the party. Maybe catch a nap.

Lana's list contains junk foods and paper goods, items readily available from any grocery. In Iron Ridge, that's Mather's Market. I grimace when I recall it's around the corner from my house. If Lana had told me what she needed on the phone, I could have stopped there first.

The size of a mini-mart, Mather's is packed with people more intent on gossiping than shopping. Eyes snap my way as I wind through the crowd. Tourist season is over, making me the lone stranger. Stage fright grips me.

"Help you?" The man behind the register

folds his hairy arms across his paunch as his bushy, grey eyebrows slam together above his nose.

Conversation stops.

I run my tongue around my dry mouth. "I'm here to pick up an order."

The man scowls and scratches the stubble on his chin. "Order?"

"For Lana Phillips. I'm her sister."

"So, you're Lana's sister. Heard you bought the old Johnston place. I'm Ed, the owner." He points to those around me. "This here's Sophie and her daughter, Terry. Sophie and Lana's girl been best friends since diapers. The guy with the cane is Harry. Lives on the same block as you. What d'ya say your name was?"

Before I can answer, Ed heads to the back room for my order. I feel my shoulders rounding forward as I force a smile for the expectant faces around me. I'm saved by Harry who launches into a story of how my home housed a bootleg liquor operation during Prohibition. "Best bathtub gin in the county, my dad used to say."

Ed thrusts a bag at me when he returns. "Chips, pretzels, root beer, buns, paper plates, cups. Didn't have birthday ones. Figured red would do. I'll put 'em on Lana's tab."

"What about candles?"

"Don't have 'em."

"Napkins?"

"No red. Called the pharmacy. Said they got some with red flowers. That'll do ya. They're checking on the candles."

"Where's the pharmacy?"

"Marquette and Fifth."

Back in the car, I unfold Lana's hand-drawn map. No pharmacy. No Marquette or Fifth Streets. I pull out my phone to do a search. No signal! I can't even call Lana for directions. Mumbling about the inconvenience of rural living, I drive up and down the central streets of town until I spot the pharmacy.

A bell jingles as I open the door. Clutching my purse in front of my chest, I march to the register. A gum-smacking teenager, her hair a frizzy sunset around her face, stares at me from behind the counter. I try out the magic words. "I'm Lana's sister."

"Oh, yeah," she says. "Ed said you need napkins for Lana's party. I figure three packs for the crowd she's having."

"Candles?" I ask while wondering how she knows how many guests Lana has invited.

The tattoo on her cheek wiggles as she blows a bubble. "Sorry. Sold the last pack to Mary McGinty yesterday for her granddaughter's birthday, but that's not 'til next week. For sure, she'd borrow you some. She owns the Best Bait on the edge of town. Lives behind the shop. Just drive west. You can't miss it."

A twinge flashes across my temples.

A police officer, who looks like he's been dipped in starch walks in. "That your vehicle, Ma'am?" he asks, pointing at my car.

"Is there a problem, officer?"

"Noticed your Illinois plates. I like to keep tabs on strangers." He arches an eyebrow as he assesses me.

Bev intervenes. "She's cool. She's Lana's sister."

I think I see him wink at her as he walks out.

Thick clouds obscure the sun, and I wish for the dashboard compass I never bought. Who needs a compass when you live in a city built on a grid? I pick a direction at random and drive. At the bottom of the second hill, I notice a police car cresting the top behind me. I keep my eye on the speedometer. While "ten over the posted speed" is an unwritten rule of the road in Chicago, I know they keep to the written law here. A few minutes later, I'm past the outskirts of town. No bait shop; just an army of pine trees guarding the road. I pull to the shoulder preparing to make a U-turn when I hear a siren, and the police car pulls in front of me.

It's Officer Starch from the pharmacy. He leans into my open window. "You're a long way from Lana Phillips' place."

"I'm looking for Best Bait."

"Going fishing?"

"I need to borrow candles from Mary McGinty."

"Turn around, go past the center of town, stay on this road for about a mile." A hint of a smile cracks the hard line of his lips. "Good luck," he adds.

Day off says the note taped to the shop's locked door. Groaning, I rub my aching temples. I remember the owner lives in back, so I walk around and spot a cottage. As I approach, I hear a crash and a woman shouting like a drill sergeant on a rant. Only the image of candles flickering atop the brownies my niece loves gives me the courage to knock.

The tang of turpentine precedes the stocky woman in dungarees who jerks open the door. She cleans red paint from her hands as she studies me. Her look says she's met worms she's liked better.

I take a step back. "Mary McGinty?"

"Yep. State your business. I don't like strangers snooping around my place."

"I'm Lana Phillips' sister and…"

"Should of said that at the start." She wipes her hand on her thigh before slapping me on my shoulder. "Bev called and told me your problem. Can't have a party without candles, that's what I say." She reaches toward the wooden bench behind her, and hands me a stained, brown bag. "Got 'em right here. See ya soon."

Back in the car, I check my watch. It's half-past four. I still need to pick up the brownies, shower, change, and drive back to my sister's.

Lana's hand-drawn map is useless since it shows the way to Mrs. Klein's from Mather's. I have to backtrack before I can follow her squiggles down Joliet Avenue, Huron Street, and Big Bay Lane. When I reach Mackinac, Mrs. Klein's street, it's closed for utility work. I park a block away and walk, heels clicking Chicago-style, hard and fast. Keeping my head down, I attempt to avoid nods and greetings from front porch loungers, but it's futile. Soon their friendliness infects me, and I find myself waving in response.

Yellow day lilies fill Mrs. Klein's front yard. Already at the door when I arrive, she ushers me inside. "You're Lana's sister for sure. Same eyes and nose."

I do a double-take. Except for her long, purple-lacquered nails, Mrs. Klein is a clone of Mrs. Claus.

"Are the brownies ready?" I ask, noting her apron free of batter spatters.

"The butter should be just soft enough for mixing now."

I blink and take a deep breath. "You haven't baked them yet?" My temples throb.

She squeezes my arm as she leads me into her kitchen. "Now, dear. Don't you worry yourself. They'll be ready in a jiffy." She studies my face. "You look pinched. Must be from living in the city all your life. Sit here and have a glass of my homemade peach liqueur on ice while I whip up those brownies. We'll chat while I work."

My heart races as I calculate how long the mixing, baking, cooling, and cutting will take. I'll have to forgo my shower and go straight to Lana's. Even then I'll be late. I call Lana on Mrs. Klein's landline to explain.

"I don't care if you're late," she says to my surprise. "You absolutely have to go back to your house and pick up Mom's glass pitcher. I dropped mine and it broke into in a hundred pieces. I don't have anything big enough for the lemonade. I know you're tired of driving around, but do it for me. Please?"

Two glasses of peach liqueur and Mrs. Klein's prattle soothe my headache. To my surprise, I'm soon calling her Mildred, and she's telling tales on her neighbors while coaxing stories of young, naughty Lana out of me. It feels good to laugh with another woman in her kitchen while she bustles about and fusses over me. Not like being at home, but homey.

Brownies in hand, I leave Mildred with the promise I'll help her put up the last of her red currant preserves. On my way back, I surprise myself by making all the correct turns. I think about the people I met throughout the day, mostly friendly and eager to help. Remembering the friends and the life I left behind, I wipe my eyes with the back of my hand. Starting over will be hard, but perhaps easier than I imagined.

I turn onto my street. Cars are crammed into every available parking space. A crowd is milling in front of a house—my house! What's happening? Was my house vandalized? Is there a fire? I don't smell smoke, and the Fire Department isn't here. Puzzled, I double park near my house and push my way to the front walk ignoring those around me. Someone grabs me and brings me to a halt. It's Lana. I clutch at her. "What's going on? Why are all these people here? Why are you here?"

She hugs me. "Calm down. Everything's fine. Look around."

I examine the crowd more closely. There's Ed from the grocery, gum-smacking Bev, and Officer Starch. Mary McGinty walks out the front door and places a bowl of chips on a table set up on the lawn. I still don't understand, so Lana points to a banner hanging over my porch. Red-painted letters spell out the only explanation I need: *Welcome, neighbor!*

Revelation

by Summer Jones
Finalist 2014 Short Story Contest

The steady, constant rhythm of the bustling street was comforting. Her footsteps were just another pair blending into the ebb and flow of mid-day traffic.

Arianna could feel a light sweat begin to bead up at her hairline from the heat, but was grateful for the sunshine that glimmered off her honey-blonde hair. Seattle was stuck in a permanent, rainy spring most of the year. The brief and unbearably hot summer somehow caught many off guard every season. It would seem half the city had the same idea she had, with crowds of people milling about the pier over the sound. Still, there was a pleasant salt-water breeze coming off the bay that cooled her from the broiling sunshine the nearer she got.

It was an unusual smell, far different from the dryness of her native Phoenix. She was amazed at the populace that were struggling with the high temperatures, when day's like this were the cooler norm in Arizona. She was tanner than most she met in the city, too, with her father's Hopi lineage playing into her easily tanned skin, facial, and bone structure. Her mother, the one she had never met, had contributed to her dark blonde hair and rounder eyes, but little else. Now her eyes, with their whiskey-brown tinge, slowly took in surroundings in this new coastal city.

There was hardly a place where some sort of art wasn't present. Spray paint, prints, stickers… the layers and layers of posters plastered over one another, advertising their workshops, book signings, music events. Her cousin, with whom she was staying, had said she would take her to an entire wall covered in gum tomorrow. She had no idea why anybody would want a huge wall of rotting, sticky, sugary goo around, but was even more amused to learn it had all been scraped off twice, years ago, and was still around to draw in tourists.

That was something Arianna didn't like thinking of herself as – just another tourist, snapping pictures and dragging screaming, sunburned toddlers. She had seen plenty of those in Phoenix, and at the cultural center on the reservation where she and her father's family had lived before. She shook her head a little, drawing herself back to the present, still headed down Elliot Avenue alone, her flip-flops slapping the hot pavement as she made her way towards the waterfront.

Her cousin, Laila, had been called into work unexpectedly that evening and had left Arianna to her own devices. Rather than sit in Laila's apartment alone, she decided to visit the EMP and get lunch while exploring. She had been a little apprehensive to venture so far from her cousin's apartment in the University district alone, but had gone anyway. She knew what she wanted to accomplish before she left the city, and was determined. She was scared she would never build up the courage to go through with her plan, and that the month she had planned in Seattle would be a waste, but quickly dismissed the thought from her head.

You just got here. Quit worrying, she told herself as she approached a crosswalk. *Besides,* she thought, *stopping in wait for the light, I have a list and a map. What could possibly go wrong?*

A few feet ahead, a young couple waited for the light while holding hands and sipping from water bottles. Arianna let out a small sigh, feeling a tiny pang in her heart. She really didn't like being alone. She felt much better when she had someone to talk to. Crossing over, she stopped at a vendor on the corner and bought a vanilla cone. Ice cream was her weakness, and the heat gave the best excuse to eat wonderfully excessive amounts of it. Letting herself get carried back into the flow of the crowd, she people-watched and scouted for a spot on the boardwalk that wasn't too crowded. Some were making their way toward the huge Ferris wheel, while others milled about the stands selling sunglasses and woven bracelets.

Her map said Pikes Place was nearby, but she doubted she'd make it that far. Turning and going down the wooden stairs, she walked across the planks and leaned on the railing overlooking the water. The briny sea smell wafted in from the Sound, and as she watched the clumps of seaweed bob along the surface, Arianna did her best to keep the unsettling insecurities that had been creeping into her head at bay.

She stayed to watch the gentle slosh of the current against the support of the planks until the sun started to slip toward the west. The rock of the waves lulled her into a sense of calm, helping her mull over her thoughts. The coming month, thinly veiled as a family visit, was her self-created chance at independent living.

She was nineteen now, taking a few basic courses at a community college back in Phoenix, but wanted to transfer her credits out of Arizona as soon as possible. She rarely left the state, and Washington was the furthest from home she'd ever been. Laila invited her to visit until she could get her own place. They decided that in the next few weeks, she would see how she liked the city and its schools. She supposed she could go anywhere, really, but thought it best to go where she knew someone. She liked it here, and was happy to be somewhere new, but had no idea how her father would feel. An only child until she was fifteen, Arianna had been her father's only responsibility until her half-brother, Caleb, had been born four years ago. She and her father were close, and she was sure he would be heartbroken at the thought of her wanting to leave.

Sighing, she rubbed her face with her hands, elbows still propped on the railing of the wharf. Somehow, she had to make him understand that she had to leave, that his family was driving her crazy. A screaming four-year-old and a stepmother who was more interested in her own new family were just two of the reasons she couldn't take Arizona anymore. Too much reminded her of what it used to be. Her father had chosen his lifestyle for the oncoming years; it was time she did, too.

Arianna had admitted to Laila that she still harbored a sense of bitter betrayal toward her father, and even more for his new wife. She hoped she could learn to let it go in time, but had to start somewhere. To carry so much resentment was to carry a giant weight chained to her arms and was exhausting, but right now, she was worried that it was the only thing anchoring her to the earth and her plan. She was scared that without it, she would placidly retreat to her bedroom in Phoenix, which would eventually turn into an apartment within her father's reach, and live within his jurisdiction forever. He had already made his disapproval of her choice perfectly clear, while Arianna had thought any parent would be proud of a child who would take an interest in cooking and the restaurant business.

She played with the fantasy of opening one of those swank, hipster-y little coffee shops she had seen all over town, and smiled in spite of herself. Running a thumb across the smoothed-over wood of the railing, she chewed her thoughts until she decided to leave, wanting to be back before it got dark and Laila began to worry.

A study of her map showed a bus stop nearby with a route that would take her home, and she set off into the throngs of people still swarming the waterfront. Crossing the Avenue again, she made her way to the bus stop with the occasional glance at her map. Finding it a block away, she leaned against the post and texted Laila, who had just returned, that she was headed home.

Surveying the street, she noticed people putting up decorations in front of the restaurants and banks. People in the apartments of the top floors were tossing wads of colored crepe paper to decorate the street. She made a mental note to ask Laila what the celebration was before she spotted a city bus at the end of the street. Sliding her sunglasses up into her hair, Arianna balanced on the curb as it pulled in and released its passengers. As she boarded, she caught the reflection of the sunset in the bus window. The doors swung shut and she let out another steady sigh. Somehow, everything would be alright.

Mad Artist

by R.F. Marazas
Finalist 2014 Short Story Contest

Doctor Vladik scanned his retina and listened for the satisfying whirr-click that signaled his identity acceptance. He opened his office-lab door, frowning. His assistant was already there, staring at the hologram painting.

Connor showed no sign of awareness as Vladik closed the door and walked to his side, standing close.

Vladik raised his voice. "Connor!"

As though reluctant to leave his trance, Connor blinked and turned his head, while his body still leaned toward the painting. "Isn't it superb!"

How many times had Vladik heard those words? Connor had collected the artist's entire lifetime output, and truly believed that each painting was magnificent. Vladik sighed. For the first time since he had brought the young man into Tempus Fugit Corporation and made him his personal assistant, Vladik began to have his doubts. This obsession with the dead artist and his paintings would be the young man's undoing.

"And just think, Doctor, today I'll see the original, just as he painted it."

Vladik gripped Connor's shoulders. "Perhaps you should reconsider. You must understand that this process is still experimental. I beg you to think long and hard about volunteering."

Connor stepped away, his eager smile unchanged. "But Doctor, we've done it. You've done it! Next year and back, and last year and back. It works."

"We've never gone this far."

"But my dear sir," Connor said, practically dancing away toward his locker, "I have a list and a map. What could possibly go wrong?" He rummaged in the locker and brought out a clothes bag. "I know everything about him. I have holo-images of all his works. I've read all the data-cubes. I know his life so well I could *be* him." He began stripping off his clothes. "I know the area, the town, the surroundings. I know every place he could possibly be. Look… I had these clothes made, the exact same clothes they wore at that time, so I won't look out of place. I can change things for the good and help him, and stop him from doing what he did. Think of it… he'll paint again. Who knows what masterpieces he'll add to his legacy?"

Vladik sighed. There was no turning back. Time travel was a reality after years and years of failed experiments. How many brilliant scientists had given their lives to ensure that the Corporation would succeed in its mission? Carson with his infernal machine exploding, set the project back years. DeGrassi, stranded somewhere in time and space, when his machine stopped working after sending him out, and all the others, until Vladik discovered the solution.

He led Connor to the chaise in the center of the room. Thin, almost invisible wires snaked from the chaise a half dozen feet to connect to the super-computer against the length of one wall. Connor settled in, his upper body raised, his head resting on the cushioned top. Vladik sat on a rolling stool and bared Connor's arm.

"Now," he said, voice low and soothing, "relax your body and mind and I'll repeat the instructions." He pressed the injector against Connor's bicep. "After the injection starts to take effect, you will concentrate and repeat the particulars of where you want to go. It is most important that you be precise. You will then begin to fade almost to invisibility but I will still be able to see a transparent image of you, which will tell me that you're on your way. Good luck."

Connor's eyes drooped and his breathing was steady as he intoned "… December 23rd, 1888, Arles France, December 23rd …"

When Connor's vision cleared, the first thing he saw was a vast field where workers were moving about. He pulled out his map and checked the co-ordinates. They were correct. He was standing exactly where he was supposed to be. Where was the town? In the silence, behind him, he heard a door slam. Wait! That must be it! He was facing the wrong direction. He turned around on the dirt path and faced the town square. The buildings matched the ones on his list. He was in Arles. Time travel was a success.

Something caught his attention at a small

building on his left. An after-image of a figure entered the front door. Connor returned the map and list to his pocket and walked hesitantly toward the building, kicking up a fine spray of dust.

The man that he followed, lurched through the brothel's door and blinked. In spite of the slouch hat he wore for protection, his eyes were bloodshot from exposure to the blazing sun, his gaunt face leathery and beaded with sweat. He thrust a crumpled sheet of butcher's paper at the woman that stood open-mouthed near the doorway. "Keep this for me," he said.

The prostitute, Rachel, shrank from his outstretched hand and shivered at the sight of fresh blood soaking the paper. "Are you insane?"

"I want you to have it." He held his head at an odd angle, which turned his face away from her gaze so she could see only the right side.

"You've argued with him again, haven't you? About your cursed art. You got drunk on wine and you argued and then you fought."

"No. He's gone away. I don't need him. He never understood what I was trying to create." He trembled. "I can't paint with this constant noise, I can't concentrate with this buzzing. Please take this. I did it for you. I love you."

"You love only your cursed art. Get out. You'll upset my customers."

Again, he thrust the paper at her, but Rachel batted his hand away. The paper fell as it crackled and unfolded. Rachel saw the object inside and screamed. "Get out, get out!"

As van Gogh stumbled out the door, blood seeped from his severed left earlobe. He pressed his hand against his ear and lurched forward past Connor, his glazed eyes looking right through him.

Oh no, Connor thought, *too late, I'm too late! I forgot to say the exact time!*

Aftermath

by Mark Trudel
Finalist 2014 Short Story Contest

"What is reality?"

The question lingered in the room like the scent from a candle waiting to be put out.

"Is reality defined as what you can sense? What you can hear, smell, taste, see or touch? Or is there something more to reality? Something beneath the skin?"

I turned over in my chair to look at the doctor and I whispered to him, "I'm not sure what reality is anymore, Doc."

The man sitting in the chair next to me smirked as he stood and began to pace the room. "And that is why you are here, isn't it? You have come seeking reality?"

The doctor had vanished from my line of sight, so I turned onto my back and concentrated on a crack in the ceiling that I had only just noticed. A drop of water hung off the edge of the chipped ceiling as if it were about to lead an entire army of water droplets into the confined room with Doc and me.

"Yes. I've lost sense of reality. I don't know if I'm awake. Even now," I muttered as I began to lift my head higher and higher, inching closer and closer to the water droplet. It mirrored my movements and came closer and closer to my lips.

"What do you see?"

"A water droplet. I see a water droplet hanging from the ceiling…" I began to panic as various scenarios ran through my mind.

"And does seeing this water droplet make the water a reality? Or do you have to *feel* the water for it to be real?" the doctor said.

Instantly, the droplet fell toward my face, landing on my upper lip. I could taste the salty freshness of ocean water and hear the call of seagulls. I felt the warmth of the sun on my skin and heard the whooshing of the waves as they crashed along the beach.

I turned to face the doctor and my face grew warmer and warmer. A tan colored substance began to engulf my vision. I reached toward it and the substance engulfed my fingers. It was sand. Frantic, I spun around and sat up, only to realize I was on a beach with the doctor standing at my side. He looked down at me and put his hand on my shoulder for reassurance.

"Relax. You are merely in a simulation that allows you to create images in your mind. You can go places you've never seen before, or create places that don't exist. The world is yours."

He pulled out two pieces of paper and dropped them on the sand next to my feet.

"Those pieces of paper will be your life through the duration of your simulation. One is a map of the area; it contains the ONLY places you are allowed to go. If you want to go anywhere, check for it on the map first. The other is a list of steps that you must take if anything goes wrong. If for any reason you go outside the scope of that map, an alarm will sound and you MUST complete all the steps on that list in order to wake yourself up and free yourself from the simulation. Do you understand?"

Cautious, I reached for the papers and glanced over them. The map was incredibly large but nearly illegible. The top half of the page was dedicated to every place known on planet Earth. My eyes glazed over all the countries in the world I had yet to visit. My eyes rushed to Spain, and then galloped across the map toward Australia, moving so fast that the map grew blurry and I filled with excitement. The bottom half of the map was an array of fictional places; some that I recognized from movies or books, and others of which I had never seen before. The images on the map were practically popping off the page, begging me to journey to them, as if I were to adopt them as my new home.

Then I turned my attention to the other paper Doc had given me. The paper was worn and dirty, as though it had been used to brew a cup of coffee. I opened it and saw a list numbered 1-6. I began to read the first entry:

1. RETURN BACK TO THE …

"Do you understand?" Doc appeared to be agitated with my lack of response.

"Yes," I said as I folded the papers and looked up at him.

"Good. Do you have any questions you want

to ask before the simulation begins?"

Nervously trying to joke with Doc, I said, "I have a list and a map. What could possibly go wrong?"

There was no answer to this question, as Doc had disappeared. I was alone.

I stood up and rubbed my hands together, trying to remove the sand, but it seemed to be glued to my fingers. I walked over to the water, and stuck my hands in; a chill ran down my body as the water rushed around me, removing all traces of the sand. I stood in awe as I admired the inherent beauty of the endless water that stood in front of me, but then I realized what Doc had said. He had told me that this was a simulation, and therefore it was not real … but it all felt so real… the cool breeze on my body, the smell of the ocean, and the sound of the crashing waves in front of me. It reminded me of a trip I had taken with some friends to Hawaii a few years back.

I closed my eyes and began to remember that vacation, as I heard the waves whooshing around me. Suddenly, a faint alarm began to overpower the sound of the waves and as I stood in place reminiscing on the trip to Hawaii, Doc's words echoed through my mind: "… an alarm will sound and you must …"

I opened my eyes and turned back toward the sand only to realize the beach had changed. I was now in Hawaii. Nervous, I looked for the papers, but they were nowhere in sight. Had they been left on the previous beach? Didn't they travel with me?

I began to panic, as the alarm sounded louder, like that of a faint ambulance slowly drawing closer.

I knew I couldn't stay in Hawaii, so I closed my eyes and thought about the safest place I could go. Slowly, I opened my eyes to see my childhood home. To most, it would appear like any other ordinary house, but to me it was special. I stood in the middle of the cul-de-sac as if all roads led to this house, my house. I had always felt safe there and so I approached the front door. As I opened it, my world went silent. The house was just as I had remembered it, and all the memories began to flood back into my mind. I thought of all the family dinners and my friends staying over. But then, the alarm blared louder and louder. For a moment, I had forgotten about the alarm, as I seemed to be trapped in a glass wall of safety in my memories, but now the glass was being shattered by the sharp siren, which seemed to grow louder and louder by the second.

I quickly tried to think of how I could get out of there, and shut my eyes once again. I envisioned my girlfriend. I was driving as she sat in the passenger's seat. This was the last memory I had of us together, but I struggled to remember what had happened. I felt something in my pocket so I reached in and pulled out a small black leather box. My girlfriend gasped with excitement.

I slowly opened the box to reveal a small engagement ring with three diamonds in the center, and the memories of this night poured back into my mind. It was the night I was going to propose, and everything was planned perfectly… but what had happened that night? My memory failed when I tried to remember.

I looked up and realized it had grown dark and it was getting harder and harder to see. My headlights seemed to stop a few inches away from the hood of my car, as though they ran into a wall of darkness outside. I nervously drove forward until I heard a familiar sound. It was the faint sound of the alarm that began to resonate throughout the car… very quiet at first… but it slowly grew stronger. I looked toward my girlfriend to see if she could also hear the alarm, but she had disappeared.

I stopped the car and sat staring at the empty passenger seat. Suddenly, white light filled the interior of the car, and the alarm seemed to grow quieter. I raised my arm to shield myself from the light and see where it was coming from. I squinted until my eyes were practically closed, but by the time I realized where the light was coming from, it was too late.

The oncoming car crashed into mine. Glass flew everywhere, and my head collided with the released airbag. Pain filled my body, but only temporarily. Senses began to fade as my world and pain began to dim. The only sense that was working was my sense of sound; the siren was louder than it had ever been.

Unexpectedly, the new dark world grew silent.

A sharp pain started at my head and continued down the extent of my body. My eyes slowly opened and light poured in. I violently blinked, temporarily blinded by the blaring surroundings. As my eyes adjusted, I began to examine where I was. I was lying in a chair surrounded by a hexagon of mirrors on every sidewall. The floor below was composed of lighting, as though I were sitting on a spotlight, and the ceiling was made of concrete with a single large crack in the center.

I began to look at the mirrors and noticed in every one, Doc was staring right back at me, as though he was my reflection. I began to have a sort of staring contest with Doc, which was only broken when something made contact with my cheek. I touched the cold droplet. As my fingers made contact with the water, I felt the sensation of warm sand and heard the familiar whooshing of waves. I turned and looked up at the ceiling to notice another drop of water protruding from the crack. I felt like I had been here before, and began to worry about my sanity.

I turned over in my chair to look at my reflection and whispered to him, "I'm not sure what reality is anymore, Doc. Is reality defined as what you can sense? What you can hear, smell, taste, see or touch? Or is there something more to reality? Something beneath the skin?"

What is reality?

The question lingered in the room like the scent from a candle that had just been snuffed out.

Striking Out

by Brenda J. Anderson
Finalist 2014 Short Story Contest

Joel Larsen rang the Jones' doorbell, straightened his teal-green bowtie and brushed the jacket of his tuxedo. The creak of the door sent his heart speeding into an interlude of sixteenth notes. He ran one hand through his dark brown, newly cut hair and forced himself to breathe.

"Hi, Joel." An angel stood before him. Samara's dark red hair was gathered on the top of her head where it burst free in a waterfall of curls. A black suede jacket accented her teal-blue dress.

"You look beautiful!" Beads of sweat popped out on Joel's forehead. He glanced down at his cummerbund and bowtie. *Teal-blue? I'm sure she said teal-green.*

"Thanks Joel."

"This is for you." Joel shoved a plastic box toward her.

"Daisies!" Samara smiled as she slid the corsage on her wrist. "I love daisies. They're so perky and optimistic."

Samara's parents came to the door to see her off. Her dad laughed when he saw them standing together. "Hey Joel, did you know that your cummerbund is a different color than Samara's dress?"

"Daddy!"

"Teal-green, teal-blue, what's the difference?" Joel mumbled as he hurried out the door. *That's strike one against the night.*

Joel helped Samara settle into the passenger seat of his little Metro and breathed a silent *thank you* when the car started on the first try. He glanced at his date. She sat looking at her hands, her lips pulled down in a worried frown.

"What's wrong?" he asked, lifting her chin with his finger.

"I told you I didn't think this was a very good idea …" her voice trailed off. She fingered his bow tie. "Maybe this is a bad omen."

"I'm sorry. No one will notice in the dark dance hall. Don't let it ruin our night. Come on… give me a chance."

Samara sighed. "Okay. You're right. We can still have a good time." She looked up at him and smiled—the smile that sent her blue eyes dancing and always made Joel's heart skip ahead a few beats.

Joel reached over and squeezed Samara's hand before downshifting for the turn onto I-10. Another twenty minutes and they'd be at the Compass Rose, enjoying an expensive steak dinner. A thump, followed by a squeal of panic, pulled Joel's attention away from the increasing traffic.

"Not again!" Joel groaned.

The passenger side window had slipped out of its hooks and dropped into the door. Samara frantically tried to protect her hair with one hand while trying to roll the window back up with the other. The handle spun in useless circles.

As the Metro accelerated, the rushing air whipped Samara's curls around her head. The black clasp that held her hair came loose, and the long locks began to fall.

"Joel, do something!"

He gripped the steering wheel. "What?"

"Anything!"

Joel jerked the car onto the off ramp, pulled into the dirt and killed the engine. He fiddled with the window, which refused to budge. *I guess this is strike two.* He looked at Samara. Though a tangled mass of hair framed her face, she didn't appear angry. She brushed away a few strands and gave Joel a look that said, *Let's see how you handle this one.*

"We have time. Let's drive back to your house and ask your dad for his car." The words escaped without his consent. He prayed she would refuse—the Metro was fine, and she could always fix her hair at the restaurant.

"That's a great idea! I'm sure Daddy will agree if *you* ask him." Samara pressed a soft kiss on his cheek.

"Yeah! It'll be fine. No problem," he said confidently. *There is no way I can ask that man for permission to drive his car.*

He trudged behind Samara as she sprinted up the walk and into the house. She held the door open, waving her hand at him.

"Come on, Joel. We've got to hurry!"

"Samara? What's going on?" Her father called out.

She bounded toward the stairs. "Joel has something to ask you."

Joel swallowed a walnut-sized lump as he faced Mr. Jones. "The window of the Metro fell down and wouldn't go back up, and Samara's hair was flying around like a swarm of bees, and then…"

"What do you want?" he growled.

Joel's stomach twisted into a square knot. "I… that is, we… um… could we borrow your car to go to the prom?"

Mr. Jones laughed and slapped his knee while Joel stood with his hands shoved into his pockets, fighting the urge to throw up. Darkness crept in on his vision – he was going to pass out, and Samara would refuse to ever see him again. He raised his hand to touch the spot where Samara had kissed him. The softness of it, and the warmth of her lips, still lingered on his cheek. He straightened his shoulders, forcing the darkness back. "Samara only gets one senior prom, sir. Do you really want to ruin it for her?"

Samara's dad narrowed his eyes. "Look at that! He *does* have a backbone." He rose from his chair, a mocking smile sitting on his lips. "I'll get the keys. But the Camaro better come back in one unscathed piece."

Joel barely managed a nod.

Mr. Jones tauntingly dangled the keys above Joel's head. The knot in his stomach tightened and black oblivion started to look good. Then Samara rustled down the stairs. Joel snatched the keys and swept her out the door.

Once again, Joel nudged the car into second as they climbed onto the freeway. Traffic on I-10 had doubled. Brake lights flashed all around him. He checked his watch.

"How are we doing, Joel?"

"We have twenty minutes."

"We're not going to make it."

"We'll get there close enough to on time."

"Take the surface streets."

He shook his head. "It will take too long. At least on the freeway we have a chance of going faster."

"A chance? We aren't even moving!"

Forty-five minutes later they pulled into the parking lot at the Compass Rose. After another nine minutes, Joel finally found an empty space.

"We have reservations. Under Larsen."

The host scanned his list. "For what time?"

"Six thirty."

"Are you aware that it's after seven?"

"Yes, but we had car trouble."

"I'm sorry, sir, we only hold reservations for thirty minutes. However, I can add you to our waiting list."

Joel sighed. "I guess that will work."

"Larsen, was it?" He handed him a pager. "Your table will be ready in about two hours."

"Two hours? The prom starts in twenty minutes."

"I'm sorry, sir, that's the best I can do."

"Well, it's not good enough!" Joel slammed the pager down, grabbed Samara's hand and marched out of the restaurant.

Outside, she snatched her hand away. "Joel! What are we going to do now?"

He shrugged. "Go somewhere else?"

"Somewhere else? Where? It's prom night for every school in the valley. All the restaurants will be packed!"

"We could go to Arby's."

"Arby's? Dressed like this?"

"They have a drive-thru."

"Joel!"

"Come on, Samara, I'm trying. Does it really matter where or what we eat? I thought tonight was about us being together."

"I don't know."

He touched her cheek. "You look incredible, Sam."

"You haven't called me that in a long time."

"What do you say, Sam? Arby's drive-thru?"

"Well, okay."

He gave her a smile that he didn't feel. *Does this count as strike three, or did I manage to hit a foul ball?*

"Joel?"

"Yes?"

"Do you know where an Arby's is on this side of town?"

"Right. Just a minute." Joel rushed back into the restaurant. When he emerged, he had a piece of paper in his hand and what looked like a torn page from a phone book. "I have a list and a map. What could possibly go wrong?"

"You mean what *else* could possibly go wrong.

What's the list for?"

"Oh, it's a list of all the Arby's nearby, just in case the nearest one is too crowded."

Thirty minutes after the prom started, Joel maneuvered the car into a parking space at the fourth Arby's and opened their bag of food. Samara nibbled on her ham and Swiss while Joel tore into a roast beef and cheddar. When he finished, he brushed the crumbs from his tux.

"Are you okay, Sam?"

"Yeah, I guess so."

"If you're done, maybe we should get going."

She shoved the rest of her sandwich into the paper bag and took a sip of her drink. "Do you remember how to get there?"

"Of course! It's right by the ballpark. There's a magnetic pull that draws all men to the ballpark."

At 8:30, Joel reluctantly pulled into a gas station to ask for directions. The Camaro bounced over the uneven pavement of the unkempt establishment. Samara refused to go inside.

"With that last wrong turn I made, we're about half an hour from the Plaza," he said when he came out. "We'll be there by nine and still have an hour for dancing and pictures."

Three miles later the Camaro shuddered and veered to the right. Joel eased the car to the side of the road.

"Did you run over something?"

"I don't think so." He climbed out of the car and walked around it. "It's just a flat. Fifteen minutes and we'll be on our way." Joel slipped out of his tux jacket and handed it to Sam. A few minutes later, he was back at Samara's window. He had his sleeves rolled up and a smudge of dirt over one eye. "Please tell me the Camaro has a spare."

A burst of breath escaped Samara's lips, and she closed her eyes. "There's no spare?"

"I can't find one."

"Now what?"

"I saw a tire place a few miles back. It might still be open."

"Maybe I should have accepted Connor's invitation."

Joel's stomach dropped into his scuffed shoes. "Don't say that, Sam. This wasn't what I planned. I wanted this to be a night you'd always remember."

"Well, you're doing a good job."

"I meant a good memory."

"I know." She bit her lip. "I guess it doesn't matter. We'd better get that tire." Samara climbed out of the car and gathered folds of teal material in her hands so it wouldn't drag against the ground. "I'm glad I chose flats instead of heels."

They returned an hour later.

"Hey, at least by losing our reservations, I saved enough money to buy the tire," Joel quipped as he pumped the jack and the Camaro slowly lifted off the ground.

Samara just stood on the broken sidewalk and watched him work. Even with his sleeves rolled up, he'd gotten his shirt dirty. He tried to cover it with his jacket. Neither mentioned the time when they finally climbed back in and headed toward the Plaza at 9:45.

At 10:15, they pulled into the nearly empty parking lot on the west side of the Plaza. The room reserved for Westview High School's senior prom was halfway through the clean-up process. Folded tables leaned against the walls and napkins and crumbs littered the carpet. Not a teenager in sight—except for the DJ packing up the last of his equipment. *This is it, strike three,* Joel thought. "I'm sorry, Sam."

Outside again, they leaned against the car. A slight breeze carried faint strains of music through the quiet night air. "Would you like to dance?"

Samara shook her head without looking up, studying her corsage. "You're like these daisies, Joel," she said, touching one of the delicate flowers with the tip of her finger. "You're determined to be happy, no matter what."

"Only when I'm with you."

She looked up, cocking her head at him. Then she smiled, her blues eyes twinkling. "I'd love to dance."

The Truth in Names

by Sarah Dayan
Finalist 2014 Short Story Contest

Raymond tucked an empty tube of toothpaste in his pocket innocently enough. Only one other person on the boat knew it was empty, except for the rolled up list with everyone's names inside. Some of the names were real, some born of lies. His own was fake, but it stuck to his skin as if he were born with it.

"Beautiful, isn't it?" David asked. He smoothed his chocolate brown jacket against himself, as if getting ready to impress someone who'd be waiting for them ashore.

Raymond looked up at the cloudless ceiling above them, and wondered if the sky in Europe would hang the same way. The tube of toothpaste remained hidden away in his jacket's pocket, just above his heartbeat.

"Remember this, David," Raymond said, more as a mentor than anything else. "Tell your children, when you have them. Tell your grandchildren, when they are born. Tell them how beautiful it was, when you left."

The shores of Egypt were gone now, miles away and behind their backs. Raymond wanted to look back when the boat eased its way out of the dock, but hadn't had the courage. The pit of his stomach always told him the truth. As the Mediterranean breeze picked up, he knew he'd never return.

"I'm not worried," David said. "I have a list and a map. What could possibly go wrong?"

Raymond's thin-rimmed glasses shielded any doubt from escaping his eyes, if only for a moment. David was second in command, only a few years younger, but full of an unexplainable taste for a life on the edge. Raymond appreciated that about him, because for every secret fear he had swallowed, David had enough outward courage for the both of them.

The trip from Egypt to the South of France wouldn't be easy. Raymond was in charge of 100 people on board, many of them only knowing him by his first name, most not knowing his last was not truly Youseff. To them, he was their lifeline out of Egypt, out of a country that no longer embraced them as its own.

Persecution had a way of taking reality and wringing out the waste until all the droplets of what wasn't needed disappeared in the ground. Raymond couldn't see his people being persecuted in a land that they had called their own for centuries, all for going to a different building to pray. He had met with people, other men who didn't feel safe staying in Egypt anymore, men who made arrangements for shiploads of Jews to leave Egypt and move to France. Raymond's family didn't know the details, but the only force that drove him to set out on his secret mission was the hope that he'd make it to

America somehow. All he wanted was for his mother and five sisters to join him.

He had to make it to the South of France without being spotted. Getting caught wasn't an option. A man in a village an hour away from the port would be expecting half of them. They would stay on his farm until all possible suspicions blew over. Raymond would take them there, and David would take the other half to a neighboring village. They would never see each other again.

Raymond had heard about America, about the tallest buildings being in New York City, about the Sephardic community that was finding its steady way to Brooklyn. His uncle was already there, in a two family house in Bensonhurst. He had wild dreams about Coney Island, and with their occasional correspondence through letters, his uncle promised to take him to Nathan's for his first American hot dog. His thoughts met his stomach and he was reminded that he didn't eat this morning for fear that his worries wouldn't let him keep it down.

Raymond leaned over the second floor railing of the boat and saw nothing but open seas around him. He crossed his arms across his chest, able to feel the softness of the toothpaste tube beneath his arms, knowing that he carried nothing more important with him. Huddles of people below stood by the first floor deck's railing, and children pushed their faces into the cooling breeze as the boat sailed on. Some were his responsibility, others were not, but they blended together for a single moment without his realizing Egyptian police were making their way through the crowds.

He pushed his body away from the railing without a second to spare. The intensity in his eyes penetrated David's and without speaking a single word, they both understood they had to move. Raymond led the way into the boat where they separated from each other and blended with innocent travelers. He picked up a newspaper on an empty chair and read an Arabic article with ease without retaining a single word of it. His heart beat against the tube of toothpaste in his pocket. The secret names of the individuals he was responsible for felt like they would slip onto the ship's deck and fall into the Mediterranean Sea.

There was not a single ounce of him that could accept the whole mission to be over, but his body felt like it was the end. The Egyptian police were onto him. They knew his birth name wasn't Raymond Youseff and they knew more secrets than he cared to acknowledge. As they marched through the second floor's interior, he feared for his mother and five sisters because the police might know where they lived.

Raymond made eye contact with a young officer, stared straight into the core of his almond colored eyes and wondered if he had a wife and children back on shore. The rocking movements of the ship cradled him in a moment of comfort, as if back on a makeshift swing near his school in Cairo, years before as a child. The police officer signaled to the others with the cock of his head as Raymond was revealed. They knew what they were looking for, tucked in the pocket of Raymond's jacket.

As the police officers continued to march through the crowds toward him, the captain of the boat approached them. They spoke back and forth in Arabic, the police insisting that they had the right to arrest him, the captain denying them because they had already reached international waters. After moments of tension, the police officers receded and never looked for him again. Raymond never learned the captain's full name as equally as the captain never learned his, but it only took a single man to free a hundred.

* * *

"That is all, *mon cherie*," Raymond said to me. A cloudless ceiling hung above us, and I wondered if it looked the same in Egypt.

"How can that be all?" I asked. "I know there is more to the story than that." I took a sip of my soda and let the Atlantic Ocean's breeze trap me in the moment.

He smiled, almost shyly. People have always told him his face is too serious, but I knew him to always be smiling, whether he showed it or not. I have only known him to be filled with truths, but his thin-rimmed glasses shielded more truth than I will ever know.

"How's the hot dog?" he asked. He always knew the right moment to change the subject, like none of it ever happened.

"Delicious. It always is," I replied.

"Did I ever tell you how my uncle brought me

here, on the second day of being in New York?" he asked me, knowing well enough that he has told me this story more than a dozen times. I didn't mind, and always let him finish one of his most cherished memories.

"He drove us here from Bensonhurst, all the way down Ocean Parkway. Nathan's wasn't the way it is now," he said.

Outdoor picnic tables filled an empty plot next to the storefront where summer beach goers, native Brooklynites, and tourists alike all came for a taste of the world famous hot dogs.

"Nathan's only sold hot dogs, that was it. I ordered just one, my uncle ordered two. We took it to the boardwalk and ate them as we walked alongside the beach. I can't even count how many hot dogs I've had in my life since then, but that one, that one tasted the best. When we got home, I wrote to everyone I knew in Egypt and told them I had finally tried a Nathan's hot dog."

I finished the last bite of my own hot dog and took another sip of soda. The world around us could have been moving a million miles an hour, but all that mattered was that I shared that lunch with him. I smiled at him, knowing that our smiles were almost identical, knowing his real name for my whole life, but only ever called him Dad.

Back Road Signs

by Cindy M. Fox
Finalist 2014 Short Story Contest

My rear end is fused to the seat just like it was yesterday. The Pennsylvania Turnpike looks interminable again and we're forty miles from the B&B, about a thousand and a half from home. Our first long road trip, and our conversations have dwindled to tiny spikes with monotonous lapses of silence. But when my husband Jim says, "Bugs don't splat on our windshield here like they do back home in Minnesota," we dig into the dirt of Pennsylvania history and determine after 300 years of farming, prolonged use of pesticides on the Quaker State's land squelched any bugs from hanging around.

No yellow and red skid marks distort our view of upcoming road signs. Travel brochures and a list of motel confirmations are neatly sorted in my tote. Famous landmarks, rich with history of our nation's independence, await us. I have a list and a map. What could possibly go wrong?

I am the designated navigator, a human GPS who is a stickler that keeps our lives on track. I'm a woman who runs on schedules. I micromanage the clock. I tick things off a list. I dutifully remind Jim that the exit to the Amish bed and breakfast where we plan to stay the night is two miles ahead, but like a deaf man with Alzheimer's, he meanders off my well-honed path into uncharted territory. After the third time circling a dusty township road in Lancaster County, I know we are lost. Jim declines my pleas to stop and ask for directions. I offer to do the asking to save his dignity, but he won't hear of it.

"No, we'll use the map for directions," he says. "That's what they were made for."

I squint through my bifocals at the cobweb of unnamed roads on the map, not knowing which one we're on. Even though the sun glares in my face, I feel like we're traveling north. I silently give up my struggle and say, "I'm hungry. Let's stop at that Amish restaurant that looks like a round barn."

Jim agrees.

After placing our order, I take a bathroom break and coming back, I meet our waitress. I ask if we're close to the B&B. Yes! She draws the directions on a paper napkin, which I neatly fold and tuck in my pocket. Back on the road, I pretend to scour the map once again and with renewed confidence tell him where to turn.

Well-rested after a night swallowed in a feather bed, we're up early for our hearty breakfast of fried eggs, homemade sausage, and towering stacks of pancakes with blueberry syrup cascading down like an erupted volcano. Farm-fresh food served by country folks make us feel like we're in Grandma's kitchen back home.

We take the advice of our Amish hosts to "go get lost on our back roads." We discover sweeping green fields, one-room schoolhouses, and Amish pedaling foot-powered carts piled high with garden vegetables every color of the rainbow. We drive past horse-drawn buggies whose passengers are cloaked in hot, black garb. I feel like an alien in an air-conditioned vehicle in the pristine countryside that is untouched by human-engineered horsepower.

Jim prefers driving the back roads as they offer more scenic views, but I have an inkling he's searching for hidden treasures, fueled by watching too many *American Pickers'* episodes. Traveling along a tree-lined gravel road into the next county, a homemade sign reads: OPEN SUNDAY & MONDAY - 9 A.M. TO DARK.

Today is Monday and the junkyard draws Jim like a magnet. Looking through the swaying thistle, I don't see any beauty in the haphazard heaps of amputated parts from discarded machinery and vehicles.

At the gate, Jim is met by a crusty old man, hands on his hips, wearing greasy clothes that look like they could stand on their own. Jim asks, "Mind if I look through your junkyard?"

Eyes smoldering under the brim of his sweat-stained cap, he says, "Dis here's my museum. Der ain't no junk here."

Jim holds up both hands in a truce. "I'm looking for old tractor parts and plows if you have them. I restore old farm machinery."

The old fellow lets down his guard when he realizes Jim isn't one of those guys who looks for scrap iron to make a fast buck. He waves Jim on. "Follow me."

I smile, proud of my Minnesota North Woodsman who told the guy what he was looking for—just like a real *Picker*. I opt to wait in our truck while Jim browses for nuggets in the piles of old iron. I have a strong urge to pee, but when two mongrels trot through the junkyard driveway, sniff the air, circle our pickup, and then wet the tires, I discard my plan to squat behind the roadside bushes.

Two long hours later, my legs crossed in a vise-like grip, Jim emerges with the owner and his carbon-copy sons in tow. He backs the truck into the junkyard and the crew loads up a rusty lawnmower and an antique plow. Now I understand why Jim was so adamant we take the truck and not the car before leaving on our summer vacation.

Back to civilization the next day, we pull into the parking lot of The Gettysburg Museum while curious onlookers survey our museum collections in the back of our pickup. In a tour bus, we circle the Civil War battleground where 200+ Minnesota comrades had been killed due to their commander's misguided strategy: Pickett's Charge. We step off the bus with lumps in our throats. Our heads bowed, we stand on the exact spot where our state's soldiers had walked into a basin, its lip firing muskets at those brave souls who gave up their lives for our freedom. Their bravery humbles our hearts and we sit in silence for the remainder of the bus tour.

After too many sleepless nights listening to semi-trucks idling in motel parking lots, I yearn for silence and am grateful our vehicle is now pointing homeward bound. To cross the Appalachian Mountains, I tell Jim my internet map printout confirms we should stay on the Pennsylvania Turnpike, which was built to avoid traveling other routes with steep grades. He opens the Pennsylvania state map which clearly shows the shortest route over the mountains is US 30, the Lincoln Highway, and insists we take it.

"Jim," I say, "US 30 is marked in red on the map. We should ask the locals if it's safe to travel."

"If the pioneers crossed these mountains with covered wagons, we can do it with our three-quarter ton Chevy truck," he says. "Besides, it has a transmission/engine braking system. There's nothing to worry about."

Thankfully, or maybe not, we are alone on the two-lane highway. Our truck gasps for air chugging up steep inclines and lets out its breath as we drop in a free-fall. My ears pop on our roller coaster ride. I white-knuckle the armrest as the truck hugs guardrails on hairpin curves. I lean towards Jim as if shifting my body weight will keep the truck from tumbling down the mountain.

My eyes are glued on the road ahead. If these majestic mountains offer picturesque views over cliffs, I don't dare look down on them. My fear escalates as the sun dips into the black forest. Panic swirls deep in my gut when I don't see welcoming lights from houses or gas stations.

Over the mountain pass, our headlights glare at sign after sign along the downward spiraling road.

Billboard-size orange signs get to the point, the consequences clear:

SLOW DOWN
SAFE A LIFE
DO NOT DRIVE IMPAIRED
STAY ALERT
KEEP ALERT
SPEEDING - $1000
RECKLESS DRIVING - 8 YEARS

And when approaching the side of the mountain:

TUNNEL AHEAD – REMOVE SUNGLASSES

And when the highway named after our sixteenth President requires maintenance, the warning sign is harsh:

HIT CONSTRUCTION WORKER - $10,000 FINE & 5 YEARS IN PRISON

Forty miles and two hours later, we coast to the end of the "Appalachian Trail" where an auto repair shop sign boasts:

24-HOUR EMERGENCY BRAKE REPAIR

My anxiety comes down from the mountain peak when we pull over to the side of the road. The truck ticks, like when the hot sun bakes the tin roof on our barn. While its high performance engine and braking system cool off, we step outside. My knees wobble and I feel like kissing the ground. But I don't. The road is littered with broken glass and body parts from dead carcasses. I cross my arms over my queasy stomach that is having a fistfight if my bout of nausea is from car-sickness or from the carnage on the roadside.

I declare a draw.

I swallow the bile in my throat and think about the back road signs that are testimonies to people who have taken drunken joy rides. On this road smeared in red, lives were lost after careening blind through a tunnel. Innocent maintenance crews were bumped off as they worked to make a traveler's journey safe. I wonder how many of those careless drivers are wearing orange in prison right now, thankful that we won't be sharing a cell with them.

Back in the truck, all is dark save for the orange light that signals our gas tank is near empty. Our stomachs are empty, too, so we pull into a truck stop, feed the truck first, and then Jim eats the daily trucker's special while I sip ginger tea and savor a bowl of chicken noodle soup.

"Jim, your shortcut took more time than I had allotted," I say. "We've missed the 6 p.m. cut-off time for checking into our motel, which I have no idea how to find."

He shrugs his shoulders. "We'll get a room here at the truck stop's motel. We'll get up early and make up for lost time."

Within minutes, Jim drifts into blissful sleep. His purring snores assure me he's not reliving our nightmare ride. I, on the other hand, toss and turn and worry bed bugs will find me a welcome host. We should be planning tomorrow's route, but my precisely laid out vacation plans are crushed and scattered on the truck's passenger side floor.

Flat on my back, I stare at misaligned ceiling tiles in the red glow from the truck stop's flashing neon sign. Suddenly, I realize some things in life don't fit neatly into a schedule. That mapping every turn in our lives is a means of possession. I feel tension seeping from my body as I wrap my arms around this new awareness.

I turn to Jim. I want to wake him and tell him these things, but they wouldn't make much sense to him, and anyway, he needs the sleep. My eyelids flutter and, for the first time, trucks idling in the parking lot don't bother me. For the first time, I feel peace of mind and the reward of letting go as I drift aimlessly into the night.

Spring Fling

Beginners

Poetry

Contest

First Place Winner

Follow the River
by Janet Lopes

Ever wonder where a river flows;
gracing meadows with water that glows?
Come on my travels. Come follow me
from springs in sand down into the sea.

I'm curving right here around this rock.
Let me deepen now for boats to dock.
See how I shape a crevice so grand;
carving steep banks; cutting through the land.

My waterfall crashes; pounce, pounce, pounce.
My water drops splash and bounce, bounce,
bounce.
Ripples to rapids, I'm moving fast;
a massive cliff guides me home at last.

Come on my travels. Come follow me
from springs in sand down into the sea.

Nature, Interrupted
by Kevin Keeney

The indigo dragonfly swoops in
on fragile gossamer wings,
alighting on a pearl white lily
suspended above the sea of green.

Bubbles churned from the waterfall
whirl on the water's surface.

Brightly colored fish jostle for space
amongst the gently rocking lily pads.

Unaware of watchful eyes,
the dragonfly dips into the pond,
laying her invisible eggs.

An explosion of water
shatters the idyllic silence.

The delicate wings disappear
into the bullfrog's maw.

~*~

Third Place Winner

Breathe in Morning Air
(A Tanka Poem)
by Diane Davis

Breathe in morning air
sweet with dewy roses' scents
a soul's soft surcease
our breaths taken for granted
until our time runs its course

White Seeds of Hope
by Marci Perrine

White seeds of hope lay peaceful and ready.
A whisper on a stem; the breeze blows steady.
The dandelion spore anticipates flight.
A whisper on a stem; a childhood delight.

A wish, a breath, seeds floating through the air.
A whisper on a stem is no longer there.
But joy it will bring in the months of spring,
as the yellow dandelion petals sing.

Sweet Cardinal
by Lisa Ann Noe

So distinguished, sits a cardinal in the light,
Drenched with the cold driven snows of white.

It grabs a twig from off the tree,
It doesn't realize, with my eyes I see.

I suppose he will use it to make a nest,
Where all winter long he'll take his rest.

The male is a beautiful shade of red,
And has a small cone upon his head.

He spots his food from in the sky,
He is quite the industrious little guy.

One lone Cardinal upon a branch,
He feeds every day here at my ranch.

~*~

Mist in the Valley
by Sarah Mitchell

The weeping mist rolls into the valley.
It is a shroud.
An unpleasant grey shroud.
Enfolding itself around every branch of every tree
it swallows the entire woodland.
Without a whisper it clings to the trees drowning
the landscape.
Like death it muffles every cry that has ever been
cried.
The early morning sun burns away the dull greyness.
The wings of wild birds
make the morning burst into life once again.

Honorable Mentions (Children)

These poems were submitted by a children's class.

My Favorite Season
by Nya Lewis

The sun is shining
The birds start to sing
My favorite season
Will always be spring
Summer is too hot
Winter is too cold
Fall is okay
But that gets old
Season to season
Whatever life may bring
My favorite season
Will always be spring

~*~

Kitty's First Christmas
by Mary Betts

A new born kitten was very cold
She danced around to warm herself
And realized the door was open
And saw a new world!
She saw something white flurry and sparkly
And put her paw in it! Brrr
It was also very wet and cold
She makes a snowman standing tall and proud
She put a hat on him and he really stood out!
Then she smiled and waved then went inside
She had her mom all cozy with pride her first
winter day was almost over
And she almost forgot to give the snowman a cover
She went outside and there was a smile that she
would never forget
At least for a while

~*~

I Sing To Me
by Kristopher Henderson-Halsey

I sing to me,
Maybe the other me,
But the other's too young
To learn this song.
I'll teach him.
Now he's going to reach them.
You're late, but I don't care.
I started without you.
Where are you?
I'm done.

~*~

Seasons
by Megan Meharra

Seasons are changing;
Winter to Spring,
Summer to Fall.
I see the beauty
In them all.

Winter's Chill,
Spring's thrill,
Summer's warmth,
And Autumn's leaves.
So amazing to see
The changes throughout the year.

~*~

Leaves That You See
by Megan Meharra

Falling leaves that you see,
So, beautiful they can be.
Colors changing in the fall;
Trees growing beautiful and tall,
Sometimes we don't see that at all.
Now that you know maybe you'll see,
All of that again next fall on a tree.

~*~

Creative Writing Institute

Creative Writing Institute is an online writing school that provides writing courses at nearly half the price one would pay elsewhere, and each student receives a private tutor. As a 501(c)3 nonprofit charity, we also sponsor cancer patients in free writing courses. In addition, we have attempted to construct our courses for visually impaired students who can use adaptive devices to enlarge or convert text into electronically synthesized speech.

Our goal: to rescue storm-tossed lives, and to escort students from their present level to their highest individual potential.

Our program has a three-tiered approach:

- We present professional material in a practical and simple method

- Private tutors personally escort students through the maze of unwritten rules and procedures

- At the end of the course, we evaluate students and recommend the next best choice on their ladder of learning

We will tailor your class to meet your needs. You will never be a number to us. We know all of our students on a first name basis. C'mon. Invest in yourself. Make it a priority. Dream big.

We'll help you build a ladder to the stars!

Courses:

- Punctuation Review
- Creative Writing 101
- Dynamic Non-fiction
- Short Story Safari
- Writing for Children
- Writing for the Middle Grades
- Writing for the Young Adult
- Fantasy in Flight
- Horror House
- Fundamentals of Poetry
- Flash Fiction
- Novel Writing Made Easy
- Advanced Wordsmithing - coming soon
- Famous Women Poets - coming soon
- Writing Programs for the Blind - contact CEO Deborah Owen

  Payment plans available at no interest.

http://www.creativewritinginstitute.com/

Meet the Team

Creative Writing Institute is the place where people come together from all over the world. We pool knowledge and resources, and make miracles happen.

Some support this ministry on a regular basis, and our hearty thanks go to them. We also have volunteers who selflessly contribute time and talents. They are ordinary homebodies, retired folks, college and high school students who want to make a difference. Most have full time jobs elsewhere, and yet they make time to help others. Our highest praise and thanks go to you.

The *Mystery Woman* planted the seed for CWI. If you read our "About Us" page, you will learn the story of how one woman, riddled with cancer and dying, recuperated and gave herself to serve others. Deborah Owen read her story and decided if one woman could make such a difference, a school could make an even bigger difference. That night, Creative Writing Institute was born.

Our team varies with life's circumstances. We pray blessings on all who have been even a small part of this work. We have workers in America, Canada, Africa, India, New Zealand, England, South Korea and Italy. God bless those who have helped in the past, are helping now, and will help in the future!

Staff Members: In 2014, we added five new tutors. Listing the newest employees first, thank you

Mrs. Phyllis Campbell, Mrs. Kim Cawley, Mrs. Emily-Jane Hills Orford, Mrs. Diane Robinson, and Mr. Joe Massingham, and very warm thanks to our charter members Mr. L. Edward Carroll, Mrs. S. Joan Popek, and Mrs. Deborah Owen, in addition to our school counselor, Dr. Helen Tucker.

Volunteer Staff: Without these co-laborers to pick up the slack in research, the newsletter, library, blog posting, article writing and social media, we would not be able to keep up with the work. Thank you, William Battis (age 90!), Julie Canfield, Deborah Blake, Jianna Higgins, Nicky Hirst, Sodiq Yusuf, Rukeme Alao, Albert Dinger, Luana Spinetti, Terri Cummings, Karen Johnson, Angela Gunn, Annette Griffin, and our *High School and College Students* – Victoria Pakizer, Ariel Pakizer, Farheen Gani, Brent Middleton, Josephine Kihiu, Sola Johnson, and NixieRose Cobler. Many others have helped along the way, and we thank each one profusely!

Jay Hirst, publisher of Southern Star Publications: Thank you, Jay, for your many kindnesses and the hundreds of volunteered hours. (Reader: If you plan to self-publish, check out Southern Star at **www.southernstarpublications.com**. They will do the hard work for you.)

God bless you, one and all!

If you would like to be a part of this work, or if you would to contribute financially, please write to **DeborahOwen@CWinst.com**.

www.ingramcontent.com/pod-product-compliance
Lightning Source LLC
Chambersburg PA
CBHW071250170626
46809CB00001B/163